FACE TO FACE

Johnny Ringo let the swinging doors of the saloon close behind him. His eyes went slowly around the room, finally coming to rest on Waco, and recognizing him as the only one present who would be worthy of his skill. Moving forward, he halted six feet away from Waco.

"Are you the man who shot Whitey Basefield?"

"Sure."

"You heard the word I put out?"

"I heard."

"And you still went ahead and drew against him."

"Man does what he has to do," Waco answered.

Johnny Ringo nodded.

"I said I'd kill the man who shot Whitey Basefield, and I never break my word."

J.T. Edson

SAGEBRUSH SLEUTH

CHARTER BOOKS, NEW YORK

SAGEBRUSH SLEUTH

A Charter Book / published by arrangement with
Transworld Publishers, Ltd.

PRINTING HISTORY
Sabre edition published 1962
Corgi edition published 1968
Charter edition / July 1988

ISBN: 1-55773-052-0

Charter Books are published by The Berkley Publishing Group,
200 Madison Avenue, New York, New York 10016.
The name "CHARTER" and the "C" logo
are trademarks belonging to Charter Communications, Inc.
PRINTED IN THE UNITED STATES OF AMERICA

10   9   8   7   6   5   4   3   2   1

CASE ONE

The Set-Up

The Wells Fargo stage rumbled at a good speed across the mesquite-covered Arizona countryside, following the winding trail which led across country from Tucson to Backsight.

On the box the driver swung his whip, yelled to the team and cursed at every mortal thing under the sun. The shotgun guard riding beside him was amused by the cursing and admitted to himself that for sheer inventive power the driver had few equals. Lounging back with the ten-gauge shotgun held across his knees, the guard relaxed. This was only a routine run, carrying passengers, not mail, nor, to his knowledge, anything of value. All his instincts told him there should be no trouble on this run.

"Look there, Jeb!" The driver pointed ahead as they slowed down to round a corner in the trail.

A girl lay at the side of the trail, face down and still.

Nearby a horse stood with reins hanging loose, telling of how the girl came to be here out on the range. The girl wore a divided skirt, a man's shirt, and plain, high-heeled riding boots. A black Stetson covered her hair completely, so there was no way of telling what colour it was.

Even as the driver was hauling back on the ribbons to bring his team to a halt, the guard was looking around, scanning the thick brush alongside the trail. Then he lay the shotgun down and swung from the box to walk towards the girl and check if she was badly hurt or just stunned when her horse threw her. In doing this he was breaking a strict company rule and if it had been a man lying there he would never have taken such a chance. It being a woman lulled his suspicions and instead of calling to one of the passengers to get out and check things he did it himself. Worse, he left the ten-gauge with its charge of nine buckshot on the top of the coach.

"What's wrong?" One of the passengers stuck his head out of the coach window and called out the question the other travellers were putting.

The guard was almost by the girl as he turned to reply but hearing a sudden movement started to swing back round, his hand falling to the butt of his gun.

"Reach!" The girl rolled over and sat up. In her right hand she held a Colt Storekeeper .45 gun, its short barrel lined on the guard's body. "Come on out, boys."

Four masked men came out from the mesquite where they had been hiding. Guns in hand they advanced on the coach, fanning out in such a way as to cover driver, guard and passengers. They were all young men, that was plain to see, even though they, like the girl, were masked by bandanas drawn up over the lower part of their faces. In dress they might have been any of the cowhands who rode the cattle ranges, for their clothes were the sort which could be bought in any store from the Mississippi to California.

The guard stood fast, he was too wise a man to buck those odds. The way that bunch moved showed them to be fair hands at the game and he knew that his chances of beating them were almost nil. He kept his hands raised and allowed one of the men to take his gun from the holster and toss it aside.

"All right, now you gents come on out," the woman ordered, looking at the coach. "Come out in ones and no tricks."

The four men who were riding inside the coach came out as they were asked. Two were affluent-looking men in town clothes and unarmed, the third a grizzled old rancher with a Colt holstered at his side. The last was a thin, poorly dressed clerk from Tucson. He appeared scared and tried to hide behind the others.

"Hand it over." The girl moved forward, waving the first three men aside and holding out her hand to the shabbily dressed man.

"Sure, ma'am." The man took an old purse from his pocket and held it forward.

The girl's arm lashed forward like a striking snake, chopping viciously down on to the man's wrist. Her voice dropped to an angry hiss that sounded like a cat facing a hound-dog.

"The moneybelt. The five thousand dollars you've got in that belt round your waist. Get it off and hand it over."

The man gulped, his face looking even more nervous as he reached under his coat and shirt, fumbled around for an instant, then dragged out a thick moneybelt. Still looking scared he handed the belt over to the girl and casually dropped his other hand into his jacket pocket.

"Watch him!" one of the masked men shouted, his gun crashing.

The small man reeled back as the bullet caught him, crashed into the coach and went down, the Remington derringer falling from his hand. The other men stood still but the driver grabbed his reins and held the startled team under control.

"He thought the ole stingy gun would help him," the girl remarked, looking at the other passengers. "It didn't, so don't any of you try anything."

The other passengers shelled out their money with no arguments, even the old rancher. He was too wise to face such odds.

Hefting the moneybelt in her hand the girl passed it back to one of her men, who weighed it in his palm and laughed.

"Feels all fat and well filled, Belle."

"You damned, stupid fool!" The girl whirled to face the speaker. "Why the hell don't you draw them a picture instead of just naming me."

The man drew back before her apparent anger. She gave her attention to the robbing of the other passengers, then returned to her horse, holstered the gun and mounted. Pulling the short Winchester carbine from the saddle-boot she rode to the coach. Looking down at the travellers she asked:

"None of you boys know who I am, do you?"

"No, ma'am," the old rancher answered for the others, "none of us know you at all."

"That's good, real good. Keep it that way."

The masked men backed off into the brush and the girl followed them. None of the men round the stage made a move until they heard the sound of rapidly departing hooves. For a moment none of them spoke, then the old rancher spat into the dust.

"That gents," he said drily, "was Miss Belle Starr. Get that poor lil feller on board and let's head back for Tucson."

Bertram J. Mosehan stood just inside the door of the Wells Fargo office and watched the pretty woman climb down from the incoming stage. She was certainly well worth looking at. Not too tall, but with the mature curves that set a man thinking of settling down. Her face, framed by the hatless black hair, was heart-shaped and beautiful, the skin soft and creamy, the eyes liquid brown with long lashes. Her face was more than set off by her figure and its tasteful, expensive clothing. In her left hand she carried the tight rolled parasol that was all the rage, in her right hand she held a vanity bag.

Ignoring the looks every man in the office gave her, she swept gracefully and majestically across towards the agent's desk. Then her bag slipped, fell to the floor and burst open. An expensive-looking necklace slid across the floor and a roll of money large enough to choke a big horse, shot out and bounced at Mosehan's feet.

"Allow me, ma'am." Mosehan scooped up the money, crossed the room and picked up the necklace, handing both to her.

"Why thank you kindly, sir." The voice was a deep southern drawl, the sort which went with mint juleps and cotton blossom. "It was surely clumsy of lil ole me."

Mosehan watched her casually dump both money and necklace in her bag. The girl apparently did not know the value of the articles, the way she handled them.

"I wouldn't take those out of here if I was you, ma'am," he said.

"I don't intend to do so," she replied. "I'm just waiting for the next stage to Backsight and then I'll be going on."

"That won't be until tomorrow, ma'am," the agent put in from behind the counter, where he stood with his eyes on her vanity bag.

"Lands sakes." She tapped a dainty foot on the floor in exasperation. "When will I be able to get to Backsight then?"

"Noon tomorrow, ma'am," Mosehan answered for the agent.

"But where can I spend the night?"

"Trent Hotel is near here and comfortable." Mosehan looked her over. They were all the same these rich deep south girls. Take them away from home and servants and they were as helpless as new-born babes. "I'll escort you there, if I may."

She turned and looked up at him, seeing a tall, wide shouldered, sun-bronzed man wearing good range clothes. He was handsome, his eyes blue and frank, his mouth firm, shielded by the close-clipped moustache. Her eyes went down over his blue shirt with the string tie, to the brown levis tucked carefully into the tops of his fancy-stitched and expensive boots. Then went back to the ivory-handled Colt Cavalry Peacemaker in the low-tied holster at his right side.

"Why, I just can't impose on you, sir. But if you could help me I'd surely take it kind."

Mosehan saw to the stowing away of her heavier bags and took up her overnight bag, but failed to get her to leave her valuables in the Wells Fargo office safe.

On the way to the Trent Hotel he learned that her name was Magnolia Beauregard, that she came from Atlanta, Georgia. She was going to visit a cousin who lived in Backsight, the necklace being a wedding present for the cousin. From the way she talked Mosehan knew there wouldn't be a cheap crook in Tucson who hadn't heard about the money and necklace before nightfall.

Leaving the girl at the hotel, Mosehan stepped back out into the street and stood for a moment looking around. The town was busy and there was a fair crowd moving along the sidewalks, too many for a man of the open range to fancy battling against them, so he stepped on to the street.

Walking along the street, avoiding the wagons and horsemen who were using it, Mosehan thought about the girl. His thoughts were interrupted by a voice yelling his name.

"Hey, Mr. Bert, Mr. Bert! My ole pappy told me to look you up if I saw you."

Mosehan turned to look at the speaker, who was now stepping from the sidewalk and advancing with the slightly reeling step of a man who'd just had a mite too much coffin varnish for his own good. He was a tall Texas cowhand, unless his clothes lied. Six-foot-two at least he stood, a wide shouldered, lean wasted, handsome young man with curly blond hair which showed from under his thrust-back J.B. Stetson hat and eyes as blue as a June sky after a storm. Young though he was, around his waist was a brown, hand-tooled buscadero gunbelt with matched, staghorn butted Colt Artillery Peacemakers in the holsters.

"Howdy, boy." Mosehan's reply was more dignified than the Texan's boisterous greeting. "Come along and have a drink."

"Them's just about the sweetest words this lil ole Texas boy heard today," the young man answered gravely. "You, sir, are a gennelman."

Mosehan watched the young man pivot round on his high heels and teeter off to the sidewalk, swing up with exaggerated care and head for the swinging doors of one of

Tucson's better saloons. Following his young friend, Mosehan entered the bar and glanced around. Even at this early hour it was very busy, almost every table being filled with men. Looking around Mosehan saw one table at the far side of the room with only one customer seated at it. Jerking his head towards this table he made for it, followed by the young Texan.

They attracted little or no attention as they crossed the room. Some of the customers knew Mosehan as the manager of the Actez Land and Cattle Company, the mighty Hashknife Outfit. They also knew him as the man who'd been taken on to try and cut the rustling which was costing the Hashknife almost a quarter of its yearly stock. How successful he'd been was also known and men watched him with some interest. They paid little attention to the tall Texan. He might look young, but those guns were worn with the air of a master.

The man seated at the table was tall, lean and studious looking. His face had a pallor about it which might have been the result of only recently coming from the east or out of prison, or it could just be the sort of skin that never tanned. He wore town clothes, a brown suit, white shirt and string tie, and at first glance he would be taken for a dude.

"Ole Doc surely looks elegant," the young Texan remarked as he sank into the chair. His voice, though it still held the sleepy, southern drawl, was sober.

"You look like you're advertising a leather-shop yourself boy," the pale man replied, his voice also a southern drawl. "Ole Dusty'd never believe it, Waco. You wearing two shirts in one week."

Waco grinned back at his friend, bunkie and partner in many a wild adventure, Doc Leroy. Since the day Waco took lead in a fight and was left in Backsight to recover, the two had not managed to return to Ole Devil Hardin's great OD Connected ranch in the Rio Hondo of Texas. On their way to do so they lost most of their money in a fair poker game and were hired as hands to the Hashknife. For two months they proved themselves to be tophands in any branch of the cattle industry, be it roping, throwing, branding calves, good-nightin bulls or hunting rustlers. Now along with their boss, Bertram Mosehan, they were entering on yet another chore.

"It's all set for tomorrow," he remarked, injecting an apparently irrelevant note to the conversation.

"Reckon it'll work?" Waco inquired, dropping his voice.

"Sure." Mosehan leaned forward, holding down his own voice so that his words reached only to the two young men. "There's been five stake holdups so far, all the work of the same bunch. The local law can't get a thing on the gang, all they know is Belle Starr's running it."

"Now how'd they know a thing like that?" Doc asked mildly.

"One of her gang named her every time."

"Which same's why I don't see ole Belle mixed up in it," Waco objected. "I never met Belle myself, but Mark Counter knows her real well. He told me plenty about her, but he never told me she was dumb enough to let that kind of mistake happen more than once."

Mosehan sat back. "All the witnesses said it was a woman leading the gang."

"Sure, so that makes it Belle Starr." Waco had been a deputy enough times to know how much reliance to put on the testimony of stage hold-up victims. They always wanted to make it appear they'd been robbed by some really famous outlaw. "Happen the gal'd been wearing a red headband and said 'How', they'd have said she was old Geronimo holding them up."

"Couldn't be, he's in Florida," Doc Leroy put in. "Me, I thought ole Belle was surely slipping."

Mosehan looked at the two young men with a sardonic gleam in his eyes. He pulled out a sack of bull durham and started to roll a smoke.

"All right, I'll give you that it doesn't look like Belle's work at all. It could be some gal using Belle's name. The only reason you're trying to prove that it isn't her is because she's a reb like you pair. How's your side of the set-up going, Doc?"

"I've been round town plenty, flashing my roll. Reckon near on every man in Tucson knows I'll be on the stage to Backsight tomorrow."

"Good, with Pete Glendon coming into town on the evening stage we'll have the trap set. You boys know this is a try-out for us. There's a lot of political opposition to the Governor forming the Territorial Rangers, so if we don't get this gang we have to disband without ever being heard of. When he can holler keno on this bunch he'll announce the Rangers have been formed."

"You all think that pretty gal is part of the gang, and that the Trent House is the jail?" Waco asked, winking at his partner.

"Nope. She's on her way to Backsight to visit kin. You get one more reb up there and you'd have near on all the Army of the Confederacy in town."

Waco lost his grin fast. "You mean she's on the stage tomorrow. That'll shorten our stake rope some."

Mosehan nodded his agreement. He could see how having the girl along would leave them at a disadvantage. There was nothing he could do about it, for she'd reserved her seat now and would want to know why she was not being allowed to go.

"We can't stop her from going along. With any luck she'll not get too much in the way when the gang hits," Mosehan told the two young Texans. "You'll just have to hope for the best."

"And we'll likely get the worst," the studious looking Doc Leroy concluded.

Shoving back his chair, Waco came to his feet. Once more he was the slightly drunk cowhand, although he still held his voice down as he spoke.

"I'll lead down to the stage depot and keep an eye on ole Pete, trail him around. Likely somebody'll follow him."

The short, stocky man wearing the loud check suit and the Derby hat left the stage station and walked into the street. If he saw the lounging Texan by the side of the building he gave no sign of recognition, although only two days before he'd been working cattle with Waco. He was headed for the bank and was in a hurry to make it before closing time. Waco trailed along at a distance, although he knew that the following would start after Pete Glendon came from the bank.

The young teller examined the bank draft Pete Glendon put on the desk in front of him, then took it across to the manager. In a few minutes he was back, asking, "How do you want it, sir?"

"Hundreds, tens and twenties," Glendon replied, glancing around, his brick red, pugnacious face showing suspicion. "The ranchers up to Backsight and Halfway like paying in small cash."

The teller fetched a pile of money that brought a whistle of surprise from a watching man. He counted it out and watched Glendon pack it into a billfold which went under the check jacket into a specially constructed pocket.

"Are you going to Halfway, then?" the teller asked.

"Sure, on tomorrow's stage. Cattle buying for the Army, son. You keep quiet about it, though."

Glendon turned and walked out of the bank, winking at Waco who sat on the hitching rail as he went by and into a saloon. Inside a cowhand recognized Glendon as an Army cattle buyer and by the time Glendon left it was established that he was headed for Halfway to buy a herd for the Army.

By a strange coincidence every saloon Glendon visited in his round of the town found a cowhand inside who knew Glendon as a cattle buyer. By a strange coincidence, Mosehan only having thirteen men on his Ranger force, the same man recognized him several times. Even so, Glendon got the feeling that everything was going well. The word would be going round that he was headed for Backsight with money to buy cattle and he was going on the noon stage.

On towards eleven Glendon entered the Eagle Dance Hall, the best and most classy place of its kind in Tucson. He was tired and decided that after this he'd go to the room already booked for him at the Trent House and get a night's sleep.

The dance hall was crowded but Glendon managed to get through to the bar. He felt someone bump into him and a hand in his pocket. Glendon's hand slammed down fast, catching a wrist and swinging the owner of it round to crash into the bar. His other fist drove out to crash into the face of a small, rat-faced man.

The crowd scattered as a second man lunged forward with a knife in his hand. Glendon's free hand went under his arm and came into view with a short-barrelled Webley Bulldog revolver in it. The gun crashed and the knife wielder spun round with a bullet-smashed shoulder, the knife dropping from his hand.

The pickpocket lashed out with his foot catching Glendon hard on the shin. With a curse of anger Glendon swung his Webley up and down, the barrel laying where it would do most good, right on top of the pickpocket's head.

Cursing under his breath Glendon looked down at the two men. The knife-toter would be a long time before he could use his arm again, if he ever did, for the heavy Webley bullet had badly smashed his shoulder. The pickpocket was unconscious and the barrel of the gun had torn his scalp open.

The crowd welled round, talking and shouting, then two members of the Tucson Marshal's office appeared. They listened to Glendon's story and the agreement other men from the crowd gave to it. Then, collecting the two wounded men, they left after giving Glendon their congratulations on his very public-spirited action in bringing these two malefactors to book.

Talk welled up again, the band started to play, and normality settled on the room. Tucson was getting civilized, but it took more than a fight in which only one man took lead, and him not killed, to stop the pleasures of the night.

Glendon was almost ready to leave for bed when a hand was laid gently on his sleeve. Turning, he found a pretty, black-haired girl standing next to him. She was dressed in the usual style of a dance-hall girl and had a figure to catch the eye.

"My, you're tough," she cooed. "I love tough men."

Glendon beamed, called, "Wine for the lady," and turned to talk to the girl.

He found out her name was Rona and that she worked there regularly. She learned he was a cattle buyer going to Backsight the following day with cash to buy cattle. The reason for the cash, she also learned was that the local ranchers did not want to take Government scrips.

After a dance or two and a few more drinks Glendon left the girl, and headed for home. Rona watched him go, then moving from the bar she avoided the reaching arms of a drunken miner and left by the rear door. Two tall young men in range clothes rose and followed her out into the night.

Walking along towards the hotel Glendon kept to the centre of the street, the gunman's sidewalk. He knew that word had gone round about his withdrawal from the bank and wanted to have a fair chance of seeing anyone who was looking for a stake before they got to him. He was alert and watchful, his gun out and held under his coat, ready for use.

"You got a light, friend?" The voice came from just behind him. Glendon came round, the gun lifting, only to be knocked aside as the voice went on, "Bang! You're dead, Pete. Real dead."

Glendon let his breath out in a long gasp of relief, then growled, "Waco, you damned Injun. I nearly killed you."

Despite his shock Glendon kept his wits about him. He took out a small box of matches and striking one, lit Waco's handrolled smoke.

"Why sure, but you didn't," the young Texan replied cheerfully. "The bank teller pointed a young feller after you. Was on your trail for a spell, then left and I followed him to the Eagle Dance Hall. Was another hombre after you. He looked part Injun to me. He stayed with you for a piece, too."

With his smoke going Waco said a drunken and cheery good-night and reeled off on his high heels. For all of that his every nerve was working and his every sense tense. Just as he turned Waco caught, from the very corner of his eye, a movement in an alley across the street.

Moving forward, hands brushing the butts of his guns at every step, Waco made for the dark alley. He hated the thought of going round that corner, shown in clear view to anyone in the shadows, but he went just the same. The alley was empty, no sign of anyone, only a faint elusive yet fragrant smell.

Passing down the alley Waco came out into a poorly-lit back street and looked around. On an impulse he went to the right, strolling along the back street until he came to a halt and looked up at a building. A light went out in a window, but he saw the curtain flicker backwards as if someone was looking at him.

Turning to go back Waco had only taken a few steps when he stopped and looked around him again. He realized where he was now. That would be the back of the Trent Hotel. Moving back he tried to remember which room the light had come from, but could not tell, so he returned to the smaller hotel where he was staying and went to bed.

At noon the following day the stage for Backsight stood waiting to leave in front of the Wells Fargo office. The various passengers gathering ready to leave made a varied bunch. Pete Glendon was one of the first to arrive. He watched the pretty southern girl entering the building and nodded in silent approval, for like all his kind, Glendon was very susceptible to a beautiful woman.

"I surely wish you'd leave that money and jewellery with me to be sent on an express run, ma'am," the agent said. "Way you've been talking near everybody in Tucson knows about them."

The girl turned her brown eyes on the agent. They were the kind of eyes to melt a man. "Why surely you don't think they'd rob poor lil ole me?" she asked.

"Belle Starr might, ma'am." Glendon removed his hat and came forward. "Can I help you carry your bags?"

"Thank you kindly, sir." The girl turned those eyes on Glendon now. Then her eyes widened and she gasped, "Do you mean that awful Belle Starr is in Arizona territory?"

"Yes'm, so folks say," Glendon answered. "She'd rob the coach if she knew there was anything real valuable."

"But I'll be safe with you along, won't I?" she cooed back.

For a look like the girl just gave him Pete Glendon was willing to take on Belle Starr, Cattle Annie, Rose of Cimmaron, Little Britches and all their assorted men friends bare-handed. His chest puffed out a couple more inches and he escorted her to the stage loaded with her bags.

Glendon helped Magnolia into the stage and knowing the best and most comfortable place to travel, put her next to the door, then took the seat beside her. Doc Leroy, who'd been watching all this with a sardonic smile and a gleam in his eye that boded bad times for Glendon after this was over, climbed in and took the seat next to Glendon at the other door. Two more passengers arrived, climbing in and sitting down. The first was a fat, flashily dressed whisky drummer who sat down facing Magnolia and mopped his face with his bandana before starting to talk to the girl. The other was a tall young man wearing city clothes and a low-tied gun. He sat next to the drummer, facing Glendon, glancing at Magnolia then relaxed. Outside, the driver and guard climbed aboard and were ready to leave.

Around the corner came the two deputy marshals, half carrying, half dragging Waco between them. The young Texan's clothes looked as if they'd been slept in, and were crumpled up in a manner alien to him. He was singing a cowhand song in a whisky lined voice and stared owlishly round as the deputies looked inside the coach, then opened the door and dumped Waco into the seat facing Doc. He flopped back in the corner, pulled his hat down over his eyes and apparently went to sleep.

"Landsakes, is he ill?" Magnolia asked, staring at Waco.

One of the deputies glanced at her, then looked again harder and swept his hat off. "No, ma'am. He's drunk, that's all. Found him sleeping in the street and put him on the stage to get him home. He won't bother you none. Should sleep near to Halfway and spend the rest of the trip telling you he'll never do it again."

The driver swung his whip and the restive team lunged forward into their traces. The jolt took Magnolia by surprise, but Glendon caught her arm and steadied her. She regained her composure and by the time the coach left town behind she had all the other passengers talking to each other. All except Waco, who lounged back in his seat in the corner and acted as if he was asleep.

Lazing back, Waco relaxed, knowing that the attack would not come until they were well out of town. His mind, always agile, ran over their plans for catching this gang. Mosehan and the other Rangers would be leaving town soon after them, bringing a wagon and horses for Waco, Doc and Glendon. They would be ready to take a hand if it was needed, but Waco doubted if it would.

Gangs which hit at stage coaches were few and far between, for a stage coach robbery was an uncertain thing. Sam Bass robbed one and lost on the deal when three travellers proved they were broke and a fourth had only two dollars. Sam gave the man his money back and another couple of dollars to pay for a room and the other three complained that this was unfair, as they had no money at all. So Sam took a collection from his boys and handed each of the poverty-stricken trio four dollars.

This gang here was different; every time they hit they made a winner. That meant the gang was getting information from town and that they would know, due to careful planning on the part of Mosehan, this coach was carrying more than most.

The men who had followed Glendon were probably part of the gang, or one of them would be. The other . . . Waco's good friend, Mark Counter, was an old friend of Belle Starr and knew her very well. In talks around the fire Mark had often talked of Belle Starr. From what Mark told about the lady outlaw Waco could not see her mixed in with the gang. There was a whole lot which didn't tie in with the smoothly efficient way she handled herself and any men she took on to help her. There was something more Mark had told him about Belle Starr, something that would identify her instantly to anyone who knew her at all.

It was then a faint smell came to his nostrils, through the smell of stale sweat, whisky and tobacco smoke which pervaded the interior of the coach. His nostrils quivered, taking in the scent. Waco grunted, writhed round in his seat and from under the shielding brim of his expensive Stetson studied Magnolia's hands. They were gloveless and toying with the handle of her parasol, which she held between her knees. Satisfied with what he saw, Waco grunted restlessly and turned back to the window again.

The coach was once more in the thick mesquite scrub country again, for the most part travelling along a blind trail. Neither guard nor driver expected trouble this near town and they were taken by surprise when rounding another curve, holding the team down to a slow walk, they found a tree trunk dragged across the track. Behind it stood three masked men holding rifles.

"Hold-up. Throw your hands high!" a voice snapped

from the side of the coach and the woman stepped out into view, her short barrelled Colt in her hand.

Even as the coach came to a halt the three Rangers prepared to spring Mosehan's carefully laid trap. Waco still stayed as he was, but slowly his hand went to the door handle and eased it down ready to get out and into action so fast the outlaws would not have a chance to endanger the other passengers.

"Hold it, all of you." The young man facing Glendon now held a gun, not the one in his holster, but a second brought from under his coat.

Waco and Doc sat fast, the hammer of that gun was eased back and no way could they move fast enough to stop the man killing their friend. This was the first time that the gang ever used an inside man on the job and they had not been expecting it. There was nothing they could do except wait for a chance to break the hold this man held over them.

The door nearest Magnolia opened and the woman outlaw looked in, resting her gun on the floor of the coach right next to Magnolia's feet. The southern girl gave a squeal of fright and slumped down in her seat, hands flopping to her sides.

The masked woman laughed as she looked Magnolia over, then said, "Get them out of it, Frank."

The young man made a mistake then. He gestured to the men with his gun, taking it away from the line on Glendon. Instantly there sounded the crash of a shot and flame tore from the side of Magnolia's parasol. The young man's back arched as a hole appeared in his chest, the gun slid from his hand and fell to the floor of the coach.

Even as she fired, Magnolia's foot lifted and stamped down hard on the female bandit's gunhand, grinding the heel of her shoe round and bringing a squeal of pain from the other woman. Dropping her gun the bandit staggered backwards and Magnolia dived through the door full on to her. They went backwards out of sight, screaming, cursing, tearing at hair, like two enraged wildcats.

Kicking open the other door Waco hurtled out, his matched staghorn butted guns in his hands as he landed. For the first time in Arizona territory the words rang out:

"Rangers here, drop your guns!"

The gang saw Waco hurtle from the coach, followed by Doc Leroy, and from the other side Pete Glendon made an appearance. The bandits elected to fight. One brought up his rifle and gun thunder rocked the air. The dull roar of Colt guns mingled with the flatter bark of rifles and the booming bellow of the guard's ten-gauge.

Waco threw two shots into one man. Doc cut down on a second, sending him down behind the log. The third man sent a bullet through Glendon's arm before the guard centred his shotgun and squeezed the trigger. Even as Glendon dropped his gun and dived for it with his other hand it was all over.

Waco ran forward, guns ready, and hurdled the tree trunk, almost landing on Doc's victim. The outlaw was wounded in the body and gasping out:

"Don't shoot me. I'm done."

Bending over, Waco tossed the man's rifle and revolver to one side, then pulled the mask off. He recognized the man as the teller from the Tucson bank. Then Waco was pushed aside and Doc Leroy looked down at the wounded man, shoved his ivory-handled Colt Civilian Peacemaker back into the shoulder clip under his arm and prepared to attend to the wounded.

"Where's the girls?" he asked.

From the bushes where they'd disappeared came the sound of screams, thuds, squeals, and tearing cloth. Waco grinned as he started collecting the weapons.

"They're some busy."

Hooves thundered and on to the scene came Mosehan and the other Rangers. The Ranger Captain swung from his horse and looked around him, then up at Waco, who came back to meet him.

"What's all that noise?" he asked, his voice showing disappointment. "This isn't the bunch, there's no woman with them."

"I'll go fetch her," Waco replied.

Turning, he went in to the bushes fast, sliding down a steep slope and following the marks left by the two women as the fought their way down. At the foot of the slope he halted and took in a sight which did not altogether surprise him. On the banks of a small stream was an open piece of ground and in the centre of it the female outlaw was flat on her back, legs waving feebly, arms held up by two shapely knees. She'd lost her hat, shirtwaist and a couple of teeth and now had a blackened eye, swollen lip and bloody nose that wasn't there the previous night when she talked with Pete Glendon in the Eagle Dance Hall.

Kneeling astride Rona, showing a pair of attractive legs through the split of her torn skirt, Magnolia held the girl down and landed business-like lefts and rights to the sobbing girl's battered face.

"This'll teach you to..." Magnolia was yelling, her voice still a southern drawl, but subtly different until she saw Waco's arrival. Then it went back to Magnolia Beauregard again. "To try and rob poor lil ole me."

"When you all finish with her, Miss B——, Magnolia, ma'am, Cap'n Mosehan'd surely like what's left."

Breathing heavily Magnolia got to her feet and stood with hands on hips looking down at the sobbing girl. Then bending forward she grabbed the tangled black hair, hauled

Rona to her feet and pushed her towards the slope.

"How long have you known?" Magnolia asked Waco as they followed the stumbling, sobbing girl up the slope towards the stage trail.

"Known what, ma'am?" Waco's tones were mild and innocent.

"Who I am?" The young woman touched her swollen lip and winced. "I'll have to wash and change before I can go any further."

Waco did not get a chance to reply, for they came into view of the other Rangers at that moment. Mosehan saw one of his men staring bug-eyed at the bushes and turned. He was a noted poker player and his features usually showed nothing of his feelings, but right now they did. He was by the door of the stage coach and examining the Manhattan Navy revolver he'd taken from Magnolia's smoking parasol.

"What's all this about, Waco?" he asked.

"One thing for sure, this here," Waco indicated the sobbing Rona, "isn't ole Belle Starr."

Glendon, having his wound attended to by Doc Leroy, glanced at the girl and nodded in agreement.

"Her name's Rona, works in the Eagle Dance Hall. She could be Belle Starr."

From the corner of his eye, Waco watched Magnolia's face as he replied, "This isn't Belle Starr. Belle's better looking than her. And smarter. Ole Belle wouldn't have fallen for a set-up like this."

Magnolia never even looked at him. She asked the guard to pass down her overnight bag and then requested Waco to carry it to the stream for her.

"Do you know that awful Belle Starr woman?" she asked as they started down the slope.

They were out of sight and Waco's reply was not in answer to her question.

"What made you follow Glendon?"

"You did see me then?" she asked, turning merry eyes to him.

"Nope, saw one of your boys though. The half Indian boy. Later I got a smell of that perfume you're wearing. I was just too late to see you get back into your hotel room."

"Say I was thinking of combining business with pleasure." Her voice was not the tone of Magnolia Beauregard now. "But first I saw you with Mr. Mosehan, then Blue Duck told me somebody of your description was following Glendon. Later I saw you and Glendon talking in the street. I'm only a dumb lil ole Southern gal, but I can add two and two. Taken with rumors that Bertram Mosehan is starting a Territorial Ranger group and the fact that there was to be a whole lot of money on the stage, it made me suspicious. I thought I'd cut out the business and have the pleasure. If that tells you all you need to know, I'd like to wash."

Waco walked back up the slope, his doubt cleared away and his suspicions confirmed. He was pleased the outlaw gang had not been as smart as Magnolia Beauregard or they would never have fallen for the set-up. At the top of the slope he found the wagon and the dead and wounded outlaws being loaded into it. He saw his big paint stallion and Doc's black as well as a horse for Glendon fastened to the wagon. The stage coach was to carry on with its normal run to Backsight and the Rangers would ride back to Tucson.

"How well do you know Belle Starr, boy?" Mosehan asked, coming over to Waco.

"Not well, Mark Counter told me about her."

"Did he tell you what kind of gun she totes?"

"She's got more than one," Waco replied evasively.

Looking down at the Manhattan percussion-fired revolver, Mosehan felt suspicious. He waited until Magnolia returned, then asked, "Why were you carrying this gun, ma'am?"

"A southern girl has to be ready to defend herself when she's travelling among Yankees, sir." It was Magnolia Beauregard again talking. "I surely hope my Uncle Seth never hears I fought like a common street woman."

She was climbing into the coach and looked at Waco as she spoke. He grinned back at her and replied, "Don't worry none, ma'am. Your secret is safe with me."

Mosehan was about to speak, but turned on his heel and walked away. Standing by his partner's side Doc Leroy could have sworn that Magnolia's left eye closed in a wink.

The coach started forward again and the Rangers prepared to ride back to Tucson with their prisoners. Just as they started off one of the Rangers looked back after the coach and said, "I hope that drummer don't bother Miss Magnolia none. I means for her sake, after what she's just been through."

The rest laughed, but at the rear of the party Doc Leroy saw Waco was looking solemn. Then Waco turned and grinned at Doc.

"I hope he doesn't too."

"For the girl's sake?" the Doc inquired.

"For his sake. That was Belle Starr."

Doc eyed his partner for a time, then asked, "You sure?"

"Sure enough."

"How long have you known?"

"Since just after the stage started. Mark told me she used a half-Indian boy in her regular bunch. When I saw a half-Indian following Pete I never thought much about it.

Then I remembered when I smelled her perfume in the stage. I'd caught a smell of it the night before when she watched me talking to Pete. I tied the two together on the stage, and knew for sure when I looked at her hands. They were just a mite rough for a deep south girl who never worked no harder than lifting a coffee cup. There's a scar on one, she got it when she tangled with Calamity Jane up in Elkhorn City. I knew for sure when Captain Bert showed me the old Manhattan gun. Belle usually totes it with her. She aimed to rob the stage herself, but she smelled a trap and called it off. Just came along to get the gal who was using her name and getting her blamed for pulling hold-ups."

"You going to tell Captain Bert?"

"I reckon he suspects it. I'll let her get a couple of day head start before I tell him. She saved Mark's life, so I owe her that much. Besides, she's a reb like us."

Doc rode in silence for a moment, then in a fair imitation of Magnolia's deep south drawl, said:

"Why landsakes amercy, you're a southern gennelman for sure."

CASE TWO

A Rope For Johnny No-Legs

The Cottonwood spread its mighty branches over the land, standing in magnificent isolation some thirty yards clear of the wooded land behind it. For many long years the old tree had been growing here. The now departed buffalo had once rested in its cool shade, the half-wild cattle rubbed their long horns against its gnarled old trunk. Its branches had given nest space to birds and a sleeping spot for a cougar, but this day no bird or animal found rest in the tree.

Instead, across one limb lay a rope, one end tied to a thick root which had forced its way above ground. The other end was tied round the neck of a man.

Johnny No-Legs, the Apache scout, sat afork his wiry pony, his dark face held rigid and immobile, as if indifferent to the rope round his neck. He looked down at the faces of the white-eyes who stood around and did not speak. If he was to die, and hanging was the worst way an Apache could die, he would try to die well. No man could do better than that.

The white men who formed the lynching party were not the sort usually found at such an affair. Their dress was that of a city and not a Western city at that. Only one wore a gunbelt, the others being armed with either cheap single-shot rifles or even cheaper shotguns. The man with the gunbelt was tall, arrogant and clearly the man the people wanted, a leader of men. He stood clear of the others, one hand resting on the butt of his Colt revolver, the other tapped a quirt against his trouser leg with idle purposefulness.

"Let's get on with it," he snapped.

"Do you reckon we should?" a small, meek-looking man asked.

The leader of the men turned and looked at the dissenter with disgust. "Of course we should. He killed our scout and we should kill him. Anyone in the west would hang him if they were here."

The small man, who would have looked more at home behind the counter of a New England store than here at an Arizona hemp hoedown, shook his head.

"We don't know he killed Schulze. He came into camp peaceable enough this morning and he's been with us for a week without giving any trouble."

"Look, Heeley," the tall man spoke patiently, as if talking to a not over-bright child, "our scout was killed by an Indian and scalped up there in the woods. That means an Indian did it and the only Indian round here is this one. So he must have done it."

"Why don't we take him into the next town and let the law handle it, Mr. Daggert?" Heeley asked, and a few of the others mumbled their agreement.

"And be laughed at or called cowards?" Daggert snarled back. Like all the others he was new to the west, but more than that they wanted to be accepted as one of the hard men of the country. "They'll know for sure we're greeners if we take him in like that. Folks out here string up Indians and leave them as a warning to the others."

Heeley sighed. He too, wished to be accepted in the west but not on the terms Daggert wished for. However, none of the others was willing to go against Daggert's will, so he stood back. Daggert's face was a study in savage triumph as he swung back his arm. Having come out here too late for the Indian wars he was going, not only to kill an Indian, but actually hang one. The quirt lashed down on to the rump of the wiry little Indian pony and it leapt forward from under Johnny No-Legs.

A rifle's flat bark echoed the slap from the quirt, fired from the woods behind the men. The heavy bullet struck the rope where it crossed the branch and severed it cleanly just before the Apache's weight hit it. Johnny No-Legs dropped lightly to the ground, landing catlike on his feet and turning, as were all the others, to look at his rescuer.

He sat afork a seventeen-hand paint stallion with the easy grace of a born horseman. If these men had been used to the west they would have known that here was a Texan and an outstanding member of that reckless breed. They noted he was young, wide-shouldered and handsome, but they noticed it after they'd given attention to the staghorn-butted Colt Artillery Peacemakers in his holsters, the butts flaring handily to his grip. They noticed, without knowing the full significance of it, the Winchester Centennial rifle smoking in his hands. To a man who knew the west that rifle told a message. No cowhand would carry the .45.75 Winchester rifle, preferring the lighter and handier Winchester 73. Only two kinds of men in the West carried the newer and heavier model for the advantage its extra range gave them. Lawmen and outlaws.

Riding forward the young man brought his paint to a halt and he looked down at the lynch crowd with unfriendly blue eyes. It was Daggert who first found his voice, although it was by no means as arrogant as usual.

"What the hell! Who are you?"

"The name's Waco, mister. I'm a Territorial Ranger and seeing as how decorating cottonwoods is against Territorial law I concluded to stop it. So stop she is." The voice was soft and drawling, yet filled with menace as the purring snarling of a hungry cougar. "All right, what happened?"

"The Apache murdered our scout," Daggert answered in a tone which implied that all would be well now and the Ranger would give his blessing to the hanging, if not actually helping with it.

"And you caught him?" Waco studied the men, reading Daggert for what he was, as well as noticing the obvious relief in other faces. His voice held mocking disbelief that they could have caught the Apache. Then his eyes went to Johnny No-Legs and the Army saddle on the pony. His eyes narrowed as he spoke rapidly in the deep-throated Apache tongue, filling in here and there with a Spanish word when his knowledge of Apache failed him.

Daggert and the others listened without understanding to the rapid flow of talk. At last it was Daggert who could wait no longer. He broke in with an angry tone.

"What's he say, we can't understand him any."

This was not unexpected, for Johnny No-Legs at this time spoke only odd words of English picked up from the soldiers. They were not polite words at all.

Waco tossed his leg over the saddlehorn and dropped to the ground. The move was so quickly executed that it gave the watching men no time to make any hostile moves. He landed straddle-legged, the rifle held across his body but ready for use.

"Says he didn't do it. Cut him loose."

"He's lying!" Daggert roared, pushing Heeley back as the small man edged forward to obey the order.

"Mister," there was a hard edge to Waco's drawled words now, "you'll meet a sight more white liars than Apache. He's Johnny No-Legs. Al Sieber's top-hand scout. Had you hung him and the law didn't hang you, Sieber and Tom Horn both'd be after you and do it. Just turn him loose and I'll look into it."

"You?" Daggert sneered. He was as tall as the Texan, older and more heavily built.

"I'm the only law between here and the Territorial line. Get that Apache cut loose and——"

"Like hell!" Daggert bellowed, realizing that matter was being taken out of his hands and not liking the feeling. "I never heard about no Arizona Rangers."

With that Daggert's temper snapped and his hands reached out to grab the front of Waco's shirt. The rifle butt came round in a swing which carried all Waco's power behind it. Daggert caught the metal-shod plate full in the stomach. He croaked in agony as the wind was forced from his lungs and he went to his knees.

"Some folks just don't know when to get tough," Waco growled, "and I'm getting quite sick of asking for that Apache to be cut loose."

Heeley stepped forward, taking out a knife and cutting the rope which held Johnny No-Legs' hands. The Apache grunted his thanks, walked to where his pony stood, vaulted into the saddle and rode off.

"We'd best head back for your wagons there," Waco remarked, jerking a thumb in the direction of a group of wagons which were circled half-a-mile away. "This thing wants talking out."

The would-be lynch mob walked in a loose group around Waco, and Heeley told him about themselves. They'd come west, heading for the mining strikes in Arizona, in hopes of making their living. However, these strikes were overcrowded and hearing of good land to the north-west they headed that way. Now they were making for the town of Two Forks over the Arizona line in Utah, prepared to join a larger train and head west. Their wagonmaster broke his back in an accident and had been left in the last town. They'd gone on with the train scout, Schulze, who'd took on Johnny No-Legs to help him.

It was the scout's habit every morning to go ahead and look over the route for a couple of miles before they started out. None of them was a really expert driver and he'd always tried to locate the easiest route. This morning, he'd gone out to check on a wide track through the woods ahead and after a time a man went out to look for him. Schulze was dead, an arrow in him and scalped.

The Apache returned soon after the discovery of the body. He'd been sent back down trail the previous afternoon to hunt for a wallet lost by Daggert at the last camp site and returned just after the body was found.

The lynch talk had started and Daggert grabbed the Indian, disarmed him, then said they should hang him. The others were not altogether in favour, but Daggert was a forceful man and used to getting his own way.

"So you just took a rope and went to hang Johnny?" Waco growled.

"Daggert said it was what a man out here would do," Heeley answered.

"You'll get fools any place who'll do something. I reckon my partner's right when he says if there's nothing stupid left to be done some damned fool goes right ahead and does it."

The men looked sheepishly at each other, for they were getting the idea that if they'd hung the Apache things might have gone badly for them.

The wagons were thrown out in a protective circle, although not barricaded down as they would be if an attack was expected. Waco watched the faces as he rode in at the head of the lynch party and saw looks of relief on the faces of the women. The children gathered round, studying this cowhand with interest, but he did not waste any time. He'd been to the border with a prisoner, handed him over to a Utah sheriff and was now headed back to join Doc Leroy in Backsight, ready to take on the next chore for Captain Mosehan.

He attended to his horse and then made for a fire where most of the men of the train were gathering round. By the time he got there Daggert was back.

"Tell it one of you," Waco ordered as he looked at the men.

"Well, Mr. Downer here found the body," Heeley remarked.

One of the few men who hadn't accompanied the lynchers stepped forward. He was a tall, bronzed man, wearing a hybrid mixture of eastern and western clothing. His hat, shirt and the suit were eastern in their cut and style but the gunbelt, with its Colt Omnipotent in the holster, and the boots had been made by a western man who knew what he was doing. Waco glanced at both belt and boots for an instant, to confirm his original impression. What he saw gave him food for thought.

"That's right, friend," the man agreed. "I found the body. When Schulze rode out and didn't come back again I went out. He'd told me the direction we'd be going and I followed the trail over there. It led to the woods and there I found his body. I brought it in; didn't seem any point in leaving it there, as there'd be no chance of meeting a lawman out here. It's there by the wagon."

Waco turned and walked to the wagon indicated, looking at the tarpaulin-covered shape which lay by it. Drawing back the tarp he looked down at the body of the scout. He'd been a tall, lean man. His whiskery face was twisted in an expression of agony. The arrow had struck him in the centre of his buckskin shirt and he must have died in seconds. There was blood on his gunbelt and the gun still in its holster.

By the side of the body lay a bloody arrow. Waco took it up and looked it over, noting the barbed head and the colouring of the shaft. It was an Apache war arrow without a doubt. He'd seen enough of them to be sure of that. Beyond that he could tell nothing from it.

"See, he's been scalped!" Daggert thrust his way through the other men and pointed to the bloody horror that was the top of the man's head.

Something in the man's tone and attitude irritated Waco. "When I want advice from a damned Arbuckle I'll ask for it," he snapped back.

"How many coffee coupons do you reckon he cost, friend?"

"Tolerable few, I'd think." Waco glanced up at the speaker and wondered where Downer learned the range meaning for the term Arbuckle. It was a derisive name for a useless dude, implying the boss paid for his invaluable assistance in Arbuckle coffee premium stamps. "I reckon you'd best take me and show me where you found the body."

Without another word Downer headed for the horse line, while Waco told the other men to bury the scout.

Then mounting the big paint stallion Waco rode to join Downer, who was afork a big bay gelding, resting easily in the Cheyenne Roll saddle.

"You been west long, mister?" he asked, as they rode out of the circle.

"Came out with these folks, never west of the Big Muddy afore that. Why'd you ask?"

"Waal, I never saw a dude who could ride so good before."

Downer laughed. "We use horses nearly as much as you do, back east. I've spent all my life in the country. How come you're taking so much interest in this?"

"I'm a Territorial Ranger."

"I didn't know Arizona had them."

"We've only been formed a month or so." There was a touch of pride in Waco's voice. "Cap'n Mosehan formed us up. Who all had trouble with the scout, did the Apache?"

"No. They got on all right together. That loud-mouth Daggert did but he had trouble with most every man on the train at one time or another. He had a falling out with the scout about having to send Johnny back to look for his wallet."

Waco watched the ground as they rode. Amongst the many things his friends in Ole Devil's Floating Outfit had taught him was reading signs. He saw where a horse had been ridden this way in the early morning and another later, then both returned together. That would be the scout and Downer, going out singly and Downer bringing the body back again.

They entered the woods, following a wide wagon trail. There had been traffic along it since the last rains and the soil was soft, the sign easy to read. The trail turned a bend and Downer stopped his horse before they were round. "It was just around there."

They swung down from their horses and left them standing with the reins hanging down loose and advanced. Waco glanced down at the tracks. Only one horse had gone round the corner, the scout's. He saw the marks where the horse stopped, reared and where the scout had fallen to the ground. That would be when the arrow hit him, startling the horse which threw him.

Moccasin tracks led down clearly towards the man, the toes pointing out slightly. They halted and there was the imprint of a knee on the ground near the patch of blood at the end of the mark left by Schulze falling.

"Can you read sign?" Downer asked.

"Just about follow a dragged log through and, providing it's soft and I know which way it started," Waco lied. "How about you?"

"I can, some. A Fox Indian used to take me hunting with him and taught me."

Saying this Downer pointed out everything Waco had already seen, everything but one detail. They followed the tracks to where a horse had been left standing and its rider dismounted.

"Looks bad for your Apache, Ranger. Unshod horse, rider got off on the Indian side. Moccasins. That's all the Indian way, isn't it?"

"Why sure," Waco agreed.

"Reckon we could follow the tracks and see where they lead?"

"Reckon not. It would take better sign cutters than us to follow the man who made them tracks."

"You still don't think it was Johnny No-Legs who did the killing?"

"Nope, the man who did it was taller than Johnny. Look at the length of the stride," Waco answered. "A man don't have to read sign to know that. Besides ole Johnny'd never have walked that far. That's how he got his name. He always rides every place he can. Sieber always used to say he didn't have any legs at all the way he rode every place. So they got to calling him Johnny No-Legs."

Downer was watching Waco all the time, then he asked, "If it wasn't Johnny No-Legs, who was it?"

"We'd best head back for the train. See I was out here on a scout for a real bronco Apache. A bad one."

"Who?"

"The Apache Kid hisself."

"The Apache Kid?" Downer looked around at the still woods. "I reckon you're right. We should get back to the wagons."

The two men returned to their horses and headed back towards the train again. Downer kept looking round and he looked relieved when they reached open country again, although he kept his horse at a good speed until reaching the train.

"Reckon I'd best send Johnny out on a scout," Waco remarked as they rode back. "And when we get back I want to keep them folks talking or they'll likely spook. I'll tell them about the Kid and then what we've found. It'll be for the best."

"Sure," Downer nodded in agreement. "The dudes would spook if they saw a bad Indian. I'll help you."

They entered the camp in time to see Daggert attempting to regain his lost prestige and become the man of the moment again.

He was towering in front of Heeley, who faced him with a look of quiet determination on his face and a rifle held ready for use.

"And I say we should wait for the Ranger," he was saying quietly.

"Wait nothing!" Daggert roared back. "I searched the

Indian's gear and I found that scalp in his bowcase. I'm going to do what I started this morning."

Waco spurred his horse forward and dropped from the saddle between the two men. "Hold it!" he snapped. "What's you fixing in to do now?"

"Finish what I started," Daggert spat the words out. "I'm going to kill that damned Indian."

Waco never moved, his voice was low and gentle. "Go right ahead, mister, all you have to do is pass me."

Daggert started forward and stopped dead in his tracks. He looked at the tall young Texan and for the first time realized that out here a man did not start a fight with his fists unless he meant to risk ending it with guns. Waco stood with his legs apart, balanced lightly on his feet, his hands were slightly from his side, the fingers slightly bent as they hovered the butts of the guns.

In that moment Daggert knew what fear was. He'd never seen a professional gunfighter before, but something warned him that any attempt to pass Waco would mean facing one now. Slowly he tried to bring his eyes to meet the Texan's steady blue gaze and failed. He'd met his match here and knew it.

"All right." He tried to bluster his way clear. "But we searched the Apache's war gear and found a scalp."

"Sure it belongs to Schulze?" Waco asked, aware of the crowd gathering round and listening to every word he said.

"Who else could it belong to?"

"Don't ask me. Way your kind sees it every Apache spends all his waking time murdering white folk." Waco turned his attention to the other people in the crowd. "We found us some tracks out there. Looks like your scout might have been killed by a taller man than Johnny No-Legs there. A man about the size of the Apache Kid!"

"The Apache Kid!"

The three words ran through the listening crowd like a breath of cold air. Every man and woman in the crowd had heard that name more often than they liked. The Apache Kid was to these people what Vittorio and Geronimo had been to earlier settlers. There was a subtle difference between the three, though Vittorio was hiding out in Mexico and Geronimo locked away in Florida, the Apache Kid was free, on the loose in Arizona.

"Do you think the Apache Kid is about?" Heeley asked, looking round at the open range and the thick woods ahead of them.

"Friend, your guess is as good as mine. Nobody knows just where the Apache Kid will show up next. A train like this would be his meat. I'll send Johnny out to look for sign."

"You'll do what?" Daggert roared. "He'd head right to the Apache Kid as soon as he gets away from here."

"Sure, the Kid don't know Johnny No-Legs is Sieber's top-hand scout. Like hell he doesn't." Waco's scorn lashed at the man. "You talk, think and act like a man with no head. Mister, it'd go bad for you if the Kid caught you, but it'd go a damn sight worse for Johnny. Somebody has to scout and if you can't trust Johnny you'd better go yourself."

That suggestion did not meet with Daggert's approval, and he turned and stamped away towards his wagon. The other men looked to Waco for leadership with the fear of Indian attack on them.

"What do you want us to do?" Heeley asked.

"Nothing yet, gather the folks around this fire here while I tell Johnny what I want to do."

Crossing to the Apache, Waco gave orders in Spanish, for he was far better in that than Apache. He wanted Johnny to understand his orders and from the grin the

Apache gave him, he knew that Johnny both understood and was willing to obey.

Riding his horse to the wagon where Schulze's body had been lying, Johnny No-Legs reached in, lifted out an old Henry rifle, checked it was loaded, then rode out of the circle and across the range at a fast gallop.

Waco returned to the fire and looked at the faces which surrounded it. There was fear in every face.

"Now folks, I want you to sit here like nothing was wrong. If the Apache Kid is about he'll be watching you and he'll see that you're not scared. Once he thinks you are he'll come in whooping and yelling and his boys'll be walking all over you before you know what's happened. Right now he doesn't know if you're scared or not, so he'll get his boys sending up smoke and using signal flashes to spook you. Just all of you stay set and listen to me. This is what we found today, up there in the woods."

The crowd watched him, though many of them glanced nervously over their shoulders all the time.

"First," Waco went on, "no Apache killed your scout."

There was silence for a moment, then Downer asked quietly, "How'd you know that, Ranger?"

"Easily, I knew as soon as I saw the body that no Apache did it. Somebody here with the train did the killing. A man who wanted Schulze dead, a man with brains, a man Schulze meant bad trouble for."

"You mean someone the scout had trouble with, Ranger?" Downer corrected.

Daggert, who had joined the others, leapt to his feet, anger blazing in his eyes. "Are you hinting at me?" he roared.

"I never figured you in on it at all," Waco's voice cut in before Downer had time to reply. "Like I said, the man who did it had brains and used them. That let you right off.

The man who did it was smart enough to know that with a little pointing some damned fool would get rope fever. I figger he allowed to let you hang Johnny then warn you that the law would hang you if it was found out. That way there'd be no talking about it. Like I said he was——"

One of the men gave a yell and came to his feet pointing off across the range to where a puff of smoke rose in the distance. "What's that?" he asked.

"Apache smoke," Waco answered. "Set fast all of you, there's no need to get all excited. They'll let up more of it before they try and come in at you."

"You still haven't proved it wasn't the Apache who killed Schulze," Downer pointed out.

"I'll likely get round to doing it," Waco answered. "See, like I said, the man who did it was smart. He knew the west, had been out here before, to the north more. He knew some about Indians, but they were northern Indians and they're a mite different from Apaches. Johnny told me he hadn't killed Schulze and I believed him. If he'd done the killing you'd never seen hide or hair of him again. Apaches aren't real smart, like this loud-mouthed gent here, but they're not dumb enough to ride into a camp like this after killing and scalping the scout and toting his scalp off in their bow-case. So the way I saw it, if he hadn't killed the scout one of you must have. The man who did it was smart, he took an unshod horse from the remuda, went out and picked his place. He knew which way the scout was going and laid up. Then he made his mistakes. First he stood his horse where the sign was plain to read, no Injun would do that. He had to, so that if you decided to hold off for proof he could show it plain enough, so plain that even greeners like you could read it. Got off the hoss right side all right but toes out as he walked and an Injun toes in. He took the scalp and did something no Apache would ever do. He left the gun in the holster. Any Apache would give his eye teeth to own a Colt gun and ammunition for it."

"Who did it?" Heeley asked.

The other members of the crowd were listening so intently that only Downer saw the flashing lights on the rim just back of camp.

"A man who knew the west, a man who's been to Cheyenne. A man——"

From near at hand sounded a blood-chilling whoop, the thunder of hooves and shots. A man hurtled from the group, gun coming out of leather as he yelled, "Sioux, get to the——"

"A man like you, Mr. Downer!" Waco went on.

Downer turned, the heavy Colt Omnipotent lining on Waco, hammer earing back under his thumb.

"Smart, Ranger, real smart. I gave myself away, did I?" Downer grinned without mirth. "I thought you was fooled."

"Your kind always does," Waco replied softly. "You never find out until too late that other folks have brains."

"You still aren't all that smart, Ranger, that'll be Johnny No-Legs making all the noise, won't it. Well, you wasn't smart enough to draw before you called me. I'm sorry I can't leave you alive, you read sign too well for that. What was the big mistake I made, the one that told you an Apache hadn't killed the scout?"

"Apaches don't take scalps," Waco replied. "Put your gun down, you won't get away from here."

"No?"

Johnny No-Legs came round the side of the wagon where he'd made his way in a series of rushes, travelling further on foot than he had for years. The old Henry rifle came up and crashed once. Downer arched his back as the lead hit him and went down.

Jumping forward Waco kicked the gun away and bent over Downer. The train doctor crowded up but needed only one glance to know there was nothing he could do. They made Downer comfortable and Waco sent all but the doctor and Heeley away.

"I'm not smart," Downer said bitterly as he looked up at Waco. "I'd even forgotten Johnny No-Legs was out there. If you hadn't come along they'd have hung the Apache and I'd have kept them quiet about it."

"Why did you kill Schulze?" Waco asked.

"He knew me up north. I was running guns to the Sioux, only got out of the country by the skin of my teeth. Went east and staked there, but I couldn't settle. I wanted to see the plains again and came west with these folks. Schulze recognized me and tried to blackmail me. I waited until we were well away from anywhere to kill him. You read it all right. You was on to me from the start."

"Sure, you might have bought the gunbelt and saddle from somebody who'd been west. But Frank Meanea doesn't make ready-to-wear boots. He makes them to measure and it wasn't likely you'd have found a man with feet the exact size of your'n to buy the boots from. You knew too much about Indians and about western talk."

The doctor looked at Waco and shook his head. The young Texan rose and Heeley got to his feet, holding out a hand.

"Thanks, Waco, you saved us from making a bad mistake. Come and eat with me and my wife."

At dawn the following day Waco sat his paint and watched the wagons pull out. Downer died the previous evening and now lay in a grave next to the man he murdered. The travellers had voted Heeley their wagon master and he sat with Johnny No-Legs talking to Waco.

"I'll see your report of this is delivered to the sheriff in

Coconino County," Waco said. "Johnny'll get you to Two Forks and you'll be right from there."

"Thanks, you reckon things will be all right?"

"Sure, just don't let anybody talk you into doing anything foolish again. See you down trail someday."

Under the branch of the tree Waco stopped his horse and twisted in the saddle looking back. Already Heeley and Johnny No-Legs were riding fast towards the head of the train.

A bird came gliding down and settled on the bullet-scarred branch which the day before almost held the swinging body of a man.

CASE THREE

Mean Looking Man

Jack Targay rode into the town of Mecate early one morning after a night sage-henning on the prairie. He came along Main Street afork a tired bay cowhorse, lounging in the saddle and looking neither right nor left.

He was a tall, lean, though powerful-looking man, dressed in old range clothes and belting a walnut-butted old Colt 1860 Army revolver in his holster. He wasn't a good-looking man, his face was thin, hard and set in bitter lines. The high cheek bones taken with the darkness implied that there was Indian blood in him. His grandfather had been a Comanche Dog soldier, although his grandmother was given no choice in the matter.

Even as he rode he saw people glancing at him and knew what they were saying as they watched his unshaven, gaunt appearance passing. He didn't need to hear it, he knew the good people of Mecate were saying what had been said in many another town.

"Who's that mean-looking man there? We'd best have the sheriff move him on before he causes trouble."

The tired-looking bay horse turned its head towards the hitching rail and Targay looked up at the sign on the false front. It read "Olsen's Eating House." He could read it and felt hunger on him, a hunger that could best be satisfied by eating somebody else's fixings for a change.

Glancing along the street he decided this town differed little from any of the many others he'd ridden into during his aimless drifting around the west. Only the names on the business premises differed, the people were all the same. None of them had any use for a mean-looking man, no matter how he felt or what he wanted to do.

The bay rubbed its sleek nose against his cheek, blowing softly through its nostrils. The horse had been watered and fed and he was able to eat his food without worry on that score. His face was strangely gentle as he reached up and ran his hand along the horse's neck. The animal was the only thing in the west which showed any affection for him.

"I'll take you to the livery barn as soon as I've eaten, old timer," he promised.

"I tell you, Whisper, you can't tell one from the other," a mocking voice from the sidewalk jeered. "What a mean-looking cuss."

Targay sighed as he turned, for he knew what he was going to find. Three young cowhands stood just behind him, looking him over in the flat-eyed way a drunk had when he was reaching the truculent stage. However, Targay wanted to avoid trouble and holding down his anger he turned back to his horse.

"Hey, you, ugly man," the cowhand yelled. "We expects us an answer when we talks to a man. Come on, ole ugly man, you answer us."

"Look, boys." Targay turned back to face them. "I ain't looking for no trouble."

The three cowhands whooped in delight at this. The one who'd been doing all the talking swung down from the sidewalk and the other two followed him.

"Ole ugly man's all yeller, boys?" the young hand whooped. "Let's us tromp some respect for the JC into him."

The cowhand caught Targay's arm and turned him, smashing a fist into the side of his jaw and staggering him into the hitching rail. The second hand pushed Targay forward and hit him in the back hard, drawing a grunt of pain. Then Targay's foot lashed back like a burrstuck Kentucky mule, the high heel of the boot taking the young cowhand full in the stomach and jack-knifing him over in agony.

The first hand yelled, "Get him, Whisper!" and leapt forward into a punch which flung him backwards again.

The third man launched in at Targay, who twisted round with Indian speed and knocked him sprawling into the hitching rail, then back-handed the one who started it savagely. Both of them came at Targay, he fought back with all the speed and skill of his Comanche forefathers.

A crowd gathered to watch the fun. These self-same people who would have been shouting for the sheriff if the cowhands were picking on a town dweller, stood by and cheered as they fought with the mean-looking man.

Targay was as strong as whang leather, tough as they came and packed with fight savvy gained in a hundred such battles. He was sober, too, and that gave him a big advantage over these cowhands who'd been celebrating all night.

With blood running from his cut mouth Targay smashed the hand who'd started the trouble with a looping right, knocking over the one who was down holding his stomach. The last one, Whisper, leapt back, his hand going down to the butt of his gun.

Targay's hand dipped and the old Colt gun flowed from the low-tied holster in a flickering blur of movement. The hammer eared back under a trained thumb, fell, struck the percussion cap, sending flame into the charge in the chamber and a .44 calibre ball into Whisper's shoulder.

Coming round fast Targay stood in a gunfighter's crouch, his gun covering the other two hands, even though neither were in any shape to try any aggressive action against him.

"Leather it, pronto!"

A short stocky man wearing range clothes and with the badge of the County Sheriff on his vest came off the side-walk, advancing with a gun in his hand.

Targay dropped the gun back into the leather again, a hard, bitter look on his face again. He rubbed the blood from the corner of his mouth and stood breathing heavily while he waited for the words he knew would come next.

"You're going to jail, *hombre*. I don't like gunslicks in my balliwick," the sheriff warned as he closed in, watching Targay all the time.

"Run him out of town, John, we don't want his sort here," one of the watching crowd yelled and the others yelled their agreement.

"You've got the wrong man, sheriff," a soft, drawling Texas voice cut through the noise of the crowd.

John Monk, sheriff of Mecate County, turned to see who was brave enough to go against public opinion in this manner. He saw and what he saw told him that the speaker was well capable of going against anyone's opinion and backing his will to the hilt.

Two tall Texan cowhands stood on the sidewalk, undaunted by the looks being shot at them by the crowd. One was a handsome, blond haired, wide-shouldered young man in range clothes and with a buscadero gunbelt supporting matched, staghorn butted Colt Artillery Peacemakers. The other was almost as tall, though slimmer in build. His white Stetson was thrust back from his dark hair, his face was pallid with a tan resisting pallor. He, too, wore range clothes, but over his shirt he wore a coat, the right side of which was stitched back to leave clear the ivory butt of the Colt Civilian Peacemaker low-tied at his thigh.

They lounged there, eyeing the sheriff as if waiting to see what he intended to do about their statement. His eyes went to their guns, noting the way they lay, a way which made the hair rise on the back of his neck. If these two were not tophands with guns they certainly knew how to look that way. They were as salty a pair as he'd seen in many a long month.

"Meaning?" he growled as the three cowhands staggered off, two of them helping the wounded third towards the doctor's.

"The three cowhands jumped him. He went backwards to avoid trouble," the taller of the two Texans replied. "Doc and me were all set to help him out, but he didn't look as if he was going to need help, even though he was up against three men. So we stayed out."

Monk digested the words, looking from Targay to the two Texans and back again. They would be a handy trio in a gunfight, that he was sure of, but there was no sign they'd ever met before. Nor were they the sort to make any sheriff feel like going out in the street and dancing a celebration when they came to his town. He was a fair-minded man, but he did have his electorate to think about. He knew the JC boys probably provoked the fight, but he had to stick to his local people if he wanted to keep in office.

Still, it was one thing to jail a drifter, to help keep local sentiment running the right way, when he might be guilty. It was another thing again to do so with one who was innocent and had two tough witnesses who would not be afraid to stand up in court and say so.

A plain-looking woman forced her way through the crowd. She limped badly as she came on to the street and faced the sheriff, hands on the hips of her gingham dress.

"They're telling the truth, John. I saw it all from my window. The stranger wasn't doing a thing when Billy, Whisper and Hank attacked him."

There was gratitude in Targay's eyes as he looked at the three people who were standing up for him. Never before had it happened to him. The Texans showed neither friendship nor interest in the matter other than a desire to see fair play, the woman, though not good looking, seemed to radiate happiness and friendship to this lonely, embittered man.

"Thank you, ma'am, thank you kindly," he said, flushing red and jerking off his hat. "And you gents."

The crowd started to mumble amongst themselves, but talk was all they aimed to do. They'd seen the mean-looking man draw and with the inborn instinct of a westerner knew that here were two more men as good, if not better.

"All right, break it up, get on about your business, folks," Monk ordered. "I'll handle this."

The crowd started to break up, mumbling amongst themselves. At any other time they would have been against the JC cowhands, but not when the mean-looking man was involved. One of the men stopped. He was a storekeeper and an influential citizen of the town.

"Big Joe Crawford ain't going to like this, John. He'll want to know why you let a mean-looking cuss like that wound one of his hands."

"And I'll tell him when he comes," Monk answered angrily. He hated to be backed into a corner and threatened by anyone. "What should this gent have done, stood there and called Whisper's shots for him?"

The man turned and stamped away, muttering veiled threats under his breath. Monk watched him go, then turned back to Targay.

"How long before you get out of town?" he asked.

"Not until he has a meal and I've fixed up that cut at least," the young woman put in. "Come along with me."

Targay allowed the woman to lead him on to the sidewalk and into Olsen's Eating House. Monk watched them go, then turned to the other two, drew in a deep breath and asked:

"How long will you two be staying?"

The taller of the pair pulled a badge from his pocket and held it out for Monk to see.

"We're Territorial Rangers. I'm Waco and this is my partner, Doc Leroy. We'd like to see you and the banker both."

"Sure." Monk had heard of the forming of the Arizona Territory Rangers, but this was the first time he'd met any of them. Rumour was true, from the look of this pair, that Bertram Mosehan was picking the toughest, handiest men he could find. "Come on down to the bank. Do you know that mean-looking cuss?"

"Never seen him afore," Waco answered. "But I'll tell you, he's some long on patience. Had they called me half they called him you'd have needed a burying."

Monk walked with the two Texans along the street, steering them towards the stone-built bank. He did not get a chance to inquire about their business with the banker and himself, for he was stopped by three different citizens with requests that he cleared that mean-looking man out of town.

Entering the bank Monk was about to ask the two Rangers what they were doing here, but first he went to speak with the teller and came back with the information that the banker was in conference and could not be disturbed.

While they waited two more influential citizens came up to demand the eviction of the mean-looking man. The sheriff tried to read some expression on the faces of the two Rangers as they stood looking on. He also explained to the citizens that until the man committed some crime or breach of the peace he could not be chased out of the town. This did not entirely satisfy the taxpayers. Monk was on the horns of a dilemma, for although he did not wish to go against his friends, he did not want to give those two expressionless-looking Texas cowhands the wrong idea about the way he handled the law in Mecate County.

Like many other lawmen, Monk was not sure just what the duties of the Territorial Rangers comprised, or what their powers were. One thing he and every other lawman did know was that they were answerable only to Captain Mosehan, their leader, and the Governor of the Territory. Any reports these two Texans put in would be read by both of those gentlemen. That meant Monk must play scrupulously fair in his dealings now. He admitted to himself the mean-looking man played fair and had been forced both to fight and shoot to protect himself. It would not look good in a report that he ran the man out of town for doing no more than that.

The door of the banker's office opened and two men came out. The first was a tall, slim, handsome young man dressed in quiet, but expensive range clothes, the second a fat, well-dressed man who could only be a banker. No other man in the west ever managed to have the same sort of overfed look about him.

"Thanks for your help, sir," the young man was saying as he shook hands with the banker in a way that suggested he was a depositor and not a loan seeker. "I'm real obliged to you. It's good of you to go out to the spread with me tomorrow."

The banker looked up sharply and an expression of annoyance crossed his face as he shook his balding head vigorously.

"Not tomorrow. I can't take you to see the property tomorrow. I thought we'd settled that. Any day after tomorrow I'll be free to go with you."

The young man turned and walked across the room. He smiled at Monk and the sheriff rose, holding out his hand.

"Howdy, Mr. Dancer, you staying on here after all?"

"Sure, I've just been to fix up with Mr. Dingley when we go and look over the old Sullivan ranch."

Banker Dingley beamed warmly at Dancer. "The property is not in good shape. Old Sullivan was not a good or successful owner. However, all it needs is a little work to make it pay. Just a little work. Then it will be a credit to Mecate County. I'm sorry I can't go with you tomorrow."

Dancer thanked the banker again and walked out, glancing at the two cowhands as he passed. Waco watched him go, noting that although he wore the dress of a tophand he did not have the look of a cowhand. Outside the bank he was joined by two other cowhands and walked off out of sight with them.

"I'd like to see you, Mr. Dingley," Monk said as the banker turned to go back into his office.

"I'm rather busy this morning, sheriff. By the way, have you run that mean-looking man out of town?"

"Not yet. These are two Rangers from Tucson and they want to see us both."

Dingley looked Waco and Doc over with some distaste, but before he could either object or agree they were walking by him into the office. He followed, his face turning red and pompous. Then he, like the sheriff, got an uneasy suspicion of why these two young men might be in town. Both could have made a guess, even though both hoped it would be wrong.

Having no choice but to accept them as visitors, Dingley waved them and the sheriff into the hard-looking chairs which faced the big, clear-topped desk.

"Now," Dingley sat back in his chair, the picture of a man with no monetary cares and at peace with the world, "why haven't you run that man out of town, John?"

"Can't, he's not done anything wrong. The JC boys started the fight and he finished it."

"We don't want his sort in Mecate." The banker's chest puffed out as he delivered the judgment. "What we need is more presentable young men like Mr. Dancer. A fine, sterling young lad that. He deposited three thousand dollars with us and he means to buy the old Sullivan ranch. That is——"

"Mister," Waco's voice cut through and silenced the flow of praise for Dancer and the old Sullivan place. "You're holding twenty thousand dollars of Army money in your safe, over and above what you have of your own."

The result of his words was highly satisfactory to Waco and Doc. The banker's face lost all its colour and he came up from his chair as if he'd sat on a red hot branding iron. Monk bit clean through the end of his cigar and it fell to the floor at his feet, then sat there allowing the match to burn down to his fingers without noticing it.

"That was supposed to be a secret," he finally growled,

for although he suspected the Rangers might be here in connection with the money, he did not expect them to know how much was concerned.

The banker's mouth dropped so far open that only his chest stopped it from bouncing on his backbone.

"You shouldn't have known anything about it," he gasped.

Monk swore softly as the match burnt his fingers. He put it out and tossed the end into the ash-tray on the table. "That's right," he agreed, "there was only three of us knew about it. Mr. Dingley, the Army Paymaster and me."

"Took with the feller who got to know and told, the feller he told, who told the hombre who told Cap'n Mosehan, who told us two, makes a whole powerful slew of folks who've heard about it," Doc Leroy put in cheerfully. "See, the Cap'n he heard there was going to be this hit against the bank and sent us along to help out."

"When will the raid happen!" There was some slight relief in the banker's tone.

"If it comes at all it'll be before you pay the money back tomorrow," Waco answered, watching the other two men.

Again he scored a hit. The sheriff and the banker both stared at Waco, for Monk had not known when the money was to be paid back and Dingley had only received the information in code half-an-hour before. Doc was also taken by surprise, but could see his partner's guess, for they had not been given the delivery date by Mosehan.

"I only found that out today," Dingley gasped. "How did you know when the money was to be handed over?"

"Why was the money held here instead of at the fort?" Waco ignored the question and asked one of his own.

"The cattle and horse traders are going to gather here as a central point. It keeps the buyers clear of any trouble and saves them taking the money round the ranges looking for the herds." Monk answered, for Dingley was looking dazed at finding his plans all gone wrong. "I'll have my deputies guarding the bank all day. There's only two of them in town today, the rest of them are out."

"Been many new faces around town?" Doc inquired.

"A few, they come and go. Young Dancer and his hands have only been here for a week or so."

"You can't suspect him, John," the banker interrupted. "Why he deposited three thousand dollars in the bank. A most estimable young man in every respect. You can't really suspect him, can you, Ranger?"

"Me?" Doc replied, for it was to him the question had been addressed. "I don't suspect anybody. I leave that up to Waco here."

"Wait." Dingley raised his hand, his face growing with inspiration. "That mean-looking man, he must be one of them."

"Why?" Waco snapped. "Because he looks part Injun?"

"They very look of the man——" Dingley began, puffing out his cheeks. He was not used to being treated so brusquely by a mere woman.

"Did you ever see Jesse James or Cole Younger?"

"Is he one of them?" the banker yelped.

"Nope, but I saw ole Dingus and Cole both when they were in Texas that time. They're just ordinary-looking folks, man'd walk right by them in the street and not think a thing about them."

"Sure," Doc went on when Waco finished. "Take ole Sam Bass. Nice a young feller as a man could ask to meet. Just goes to prove you can't judge a man by how he looks. Meanest looking cuss I ever came across was a tophand called Kiowa. But he wouldn't do a dishonest thing nohow."

"This isn't a lone hand chore. It'll take at least two men

to do it. All the money in that safe will take some toting,"
Waco remarked. He went to the window and looked across
the small street to a line of neat looking houses. "Who
lives over there?"

"One's mine. The next to it belongs to Miss Olsen from
the Eating House. That's the two right opposite."

"Should be all right then." Waco turned and set his hat
right, walking to the door. "You leave your deputies here,
Sheriff, Doc and I'll take a walk round town and see if
there's anybody we know."

"Sure." Monk was beginning to warm to these two
young men from Texas. He could see they'd be of the
greatest use if the attempt on the bank happened. "I'd ask
you to eat with me, come noon, but the wife's away for a
few days and I'm using the Eating House. Since Mary got
her leg burned saving those kids she hasn't been able to do
the cooking and her old Chinese cook ain't wuth a cuss.
Still, if you'd like to come along and chance it you're welcome to."

"Couldn't be any worse than ole Doc's fixings, and
mine's worse," Waco replied. "We'll be there about noon."

The two Rangers made their tour of the town, visiting
the stores, saloons and livery barn, and talking with people, but they saw no one whose face had become familiar
to them on wanted posters. In one saloon they saw two of
the men who'd been in the fight talking to a big, burly man
who had the look of a prosperous rancher.

At noon they were back at the bank and found it closing
for lunch. One deputy was inside with a shotgun on his
knees. Waco and Doc waited until Monk gave the man
orders to allow no one inside, then they walked along to
the Eating House. Monk told them of the girl who owned
it. She'd gone into a burning house to rescue two children
and was badly burned. That was why the folk of the town

and the visiting ranch crews gave her their custom, for the food was not good.

Despite poor food the Eating House was busy when the three men entered. Two waitresses in plain black dresses and clean white aprons moved amongst the tables, hurrying with orders. The tables themselves each had a clean cloth on them and the place looked far more clean and tidy than was usual in a cattle town.

Mary Olsen limped across to their table as the three men sat down. She was the young woman who'd spoken for the mean-looking man out there in the street. Looking at her, Waco wondered where the man was now.

The sheriff ordered three cowhand specials for them, remarking after the young woman walked towards the kitchen, that they might as well have this, as it was the lesser of the various evils old Wong perpetrated.

One of the waitresses brought the food. The cowhand special turned out to be thick son-of-a-bitch stew, made from the brains, sweetbreads and other portions from a calf, mixed with potatoes, onions, tomatoes and every other thing the cook could lay hand on, then cooked until, in range parlance, "You couldn't tell what nothing in it was."

The two young Texans sniffed like hound-dogs hit coon scent, then tucked into the food with all the strength of healthy young appetites to back them up. They found the food far better than they'd expected from the sheriff's gloomy predictions and saw that the other customers were also eating with great relish.

A tall shape looked up at the side of the table and a deep voice growled, "I want a word with you, John."

Looking up, the sheriff nodded a greeting and he swallowed a mouthful of the stew. "Thought you would, Joe."

Waco and Doc studied the man. It was the same who'd

been talking to the two cowhands in the saloon. They read the signs right, he was a prosperous rancher. A man who'd driven his way up through the cattle business by guts, drive and hard work.

"You run that mean-looking cuss out of town yet?" he asked.

"Nope, he's still here as far as I know. Your boys started the trouble and I've got nothing against him."

"I have. No gunslick burns down one of my hands and gets away with it," Big Joe Crawford growled. "You just tell him that when you see him."

"Mister," Waco cut in, his soft drawled words bringing Crawford's attention to him. "The man who matches lead with that dark man's buying grief."

"There's folk say that about me, too, boy," Crawford replied.

Waco could see there was no bluster about this big man. He would back up his crew right or wrong, giving them the same loyalty they gave him.

Suddenly a change came over Crawford's face. His nostrils quivered and he looked down at the plate of stew in front of the sheriff. Pulling out a chair he sat down and bawled for one of the waitresses to come over. From the speed and the smile on her face Waco gathered that Crawford was an honoured guest here.

"Lucy gal," Crawford boomed. "Go get me one of those plates of stew. Ole Wong has surely improved."

"Wong?" the girl replied, then she laughed. "We've got a new cook. Old Wong was too drunk to work this morning."

"New cook!" Crawford slapped a hand on the table in exasperation. "Don't I have the luck. A good cook comes to town and I let Miz Mary get him first." He paused, eyeing the plate in front of the sheriff. "John, is that stew as good as it looks?"

"Better," the sheriff replied. "What do you aim to do about that man?"

"I've passed my word. If he stays in town him and me'll lock horns."

The waitress returned with the plate of stew and Crawford settled down to eat it. He forgot the mean-looking man and every other thing as he savoured each tasty mouthful like a man in a dream. Crawford was a trencherman of note; he put three plates of stew away in short order, then settled down to eat a pile of flapjacks. Slapping his hands on his stomach he leaned back and regarded the other three.

"With a cook like this I'd die happy."

"You'd die hawgfat," Monk corrected.

"Can't think of a better way to go."

Mary Olsen watched her place filling as word was passed by the customers who had fed already, about the excellence of the food. She sent for another girl who occasionally helped out as a waitress and was kept busy at the cash desk until Lucy came to tell her more flour was needed in the kitchen.

"Take care of the desk," Mary said to the girl. "I'll go and fix it."

Mary crossed the room, receiving compliments on the cooking and pushed open the door into the kitchen. It looked much cleaner and neater than when old Wong bumbled his half-drunk myopic way around.

At the stove Jack Targay glanced at the stew pot, then turned as Mary came up to him.

"They wanting to close you down yet, ma'am?" he asked.

"You stop being so bitter, Jack," Mary replied. "Why, everyone is saying how good the food is."

"They don't know I'm the cook. You'll soon hear them change their bellow when they do."

Mary looked at the dark man and shook her head. When Wong was found dead drunk and Targay offered to lend a hand she allowed him out of kindness, not wanting to hurt his feelings. It took her just five minutes to realize that in Targay she had found a first-rate cook. She offered to give him a permanent job, not out of any feeling of pity, but because he was the sort of cook she needed. All too well she knew the poor quality of Wong's work and that business could not hold up unless a change was made.

"They won't. Not even Joe Crawford. I'll have a talk to him as soon as I get a chance. He'll listen to me." Mary remembered why she'd come in. "Jack, Old Wong left a sack of flour at my house instead of bringing it down here. Do you think you could come with me and carry it back?"

"Sure." Targay removed his apron and crossed to take his gunbelt down from near the door.

Before Mary could object to taking a gun along a waitress came in, her face flushed with exertion. "Jack, they're eating everything I put in front of them out there. Have you any more flapjacks cooked?"

Targay waved to the stove, "Only that pile there. I can't make any more until I get the flour. There's a stew in that pot, don't push it any further on the stove. That order of steak is ready and the coffee's in the pot. I'll be back as soon as I can with the flour."

Mary and Targay walked together along the back street towards her house. They, or rather, he, talked as they walked. Talked as only a lonely man can talk when he finds a sympathetic ear. She learned why he was so bitter in that short walk. Every time he took a riding chore someone would start trouble with him and always he was blamed for it. Rather than kill someone he'd given up job after job, always drifting and trying to find somewhere to settle down. He admitted that at times, driven by hunger, he'd taken on chores where a gun was the chief asset, but he never held such a job for longer than he needed.

Mary looked at the dark face, it wasn't handsome and the bitter lines made it worse. Yet it was not a vicious face and the man himself was quite gentle. She'd seen the way he handled his horse and the way he treated herself and the girls. More than ever she knew she must see Joe Crawford and prevent his causing trouble for Targay and give the dark man his chance in this town.

They were nearing her house now and she pointed to three horses standing at the picket fence.

"I wonder who they belong to," she said.

Targay looked at the horses, too, noticing that they were not tied but stood with the reins thrown over the hitching rail outside the fence. That was a trick few men took time to train a horse to do, not even a useful trick for the average man.

It was then Targay saw where they were. At the back of the bank. Those three horses were fastened outlaw style, standing loose, ready for a rapid departure from town. The pattern fell into place and his Indian blood stirred uneasily as it sensed trouble in the air.

"Get into the house, Miss Mary, Pronto!"

Almost as he finished speaking there was a dull booming roar from the inside of the bank and the windows shattered open with concussion of an explosion. Targay pushed the girl behind him and brought the old Army Colt out ready.

The door at the rear of the bank opened, Dancer and his two men came out, each carrying a large wheatsack in one hand and a gun in the other. Even as they started forward another man staggered out and fell into the street. Mary recognized him as one of Monk's deputies.

Then the three men saw Targay standing between them and their horses.

"Move, ugly man!" Dancer hissed.

"Drop it, all of you!" Targay ordered, his gun lifting fast.

The three outlaws skidded to a halt, guns coming up but faster than they could move, Targay was into action. The old gun bucked, throwing a bullet into the man at Dancer's right. The young outlaw screamed and spun round as the shattering impact of the bullet ripped through him. His scream put off the other two and their first shots went wild, throwing up geysers of dirt to the side of Targay as he fired again. The man at Dancer's left went over backwards, a bullet in the chest. It was then Dancer's hand fanned across, driving back the hammer and sending shots out fast.

Fanning could be done and done accurately, but it took a master gunhand to do it, and Dancer was no master. With only one shot left he had not put a bullet near to Targay. All he had done was cause Targay to miss with a shot. Targay lined and let the hammer drop. A dull click rewarded his efforts, the cap in the nipple of his last loaded chamber failed to fire.

Dancer looked at the man, then at the horses. They'd stood still for the explosion in the bank, but the shooting spooked them. Two were running now, but by some chance the third was caught up and could not get free. That was his only chance of escape, for he could hear shouts and knew that soon men would arrive to investigate the shooting.

"All right, ugly man," Dancer moved round slowly until

he could see Mary shielded behind the big man. "Move or I'll drop the woman."

Had he tried for the rest of his life Dancer couldn't have found a worse thing to say. Targay gave a snarl that sounded like that of a hungry grizzly bear looking at a fat sheep. He moved with the speed only a Comanche could attain. The useless revolver left his hand, hurled hard straight at Dancer's face and he followed it with a bound that would have made a cougar green with envy.

Dancer saw the two-and-a-half pound revolver hurling at his handsome face and jerked up his arm. Then a heavy body crashed into him, a hand gripped his wrist and crushed it. The revolver went off, sending the bullet into the air. Then he was on his back with a powerful knee rammed into his chest and two hands locked at his throat choking him. He was like a baby in that grip.

Targay's face was dark with anger as he smashed Dancer's head against the ground, all the time snarling:

"Try and hurt Miz Mary will you!"

Mary saw men running round the side of the bank and gasped out, "Let him loose, Jack. Stop it!"

Slowly the big hands relaxed and Targay got to his feet, looking at the two Texans who'd spoken up for him that morning. Waco and Doc halted, holstering their guns and looking round.

"All right, friend, we'll take care of things now," Waco said, grinning wryly at Targay. "And thanks."

Other men were crowding round now, talking loudly.

"You called it right, Waco. There was a hit."

Targay got to his feet seeing accusing looks on the faces of some of the men in the crowd. Then Mary was before him, her face showing the contempt she felt for these men who were ready to accuse Jack Targay just because of his looks.

"Yes!" her voice lashed at the men, making them writhe. "The bank was robbed and Jack Targay stopped the men who did it. He stopped three of them."

The banker came puffing up, having run for a greater distance than he'd found necessary in many a year. He stopped and his reddened face went almost purple as he saw the bags.

"A fine thing," he gasped out. "A fine thing. Two Rangers and the County Sheriff's office and I still get robbed." He glared at Dancer, then up at Targay. "I owe you my deepest thanks, sir."

Monk looked at the two Rangers, then at his deputy, who was being attended to by the town doctor. For a moment he was silent, then he said:

"We surely missed out this time."

Waco's grin was a trifle weak as he replied, "You're the one who needs to worry. Come election time we'll be long gone from here."

The crowd was growing fast and Waco saw that men who'd been wanting Targay run out of town were now slapping him on the back like he was a rich uncle.

Then Crawford and his two men forced their way through the crowd. The big rancher glanced down at the two wounded outlaws and brought his gaze to rest on the mean-looking man.

"You the man who gunned down my hand?" he asked.

Targay let out his breath in a sigh. He knew the sort of man Crawford was. The rancher might be grateful to him for stopping the bank robbery but it would not stop him trying to avenge the shooting of one of his men. This would be the end of all Targay's hopes, his actions might have let him settle down here but he would not kill a man like Crawford to do so.

"Mister, this town ain't big enough for me and a gun-slick who downs one of my hands," Crawford growled, hand hovering the butt of his gun. "I'll give you——"

Lucy came running up, pushing in between the two men and looking at Targay.

"Jack, please hurry with the flour. We're running short of everything and Joe Crawford wants some more of your flapjacks when he gets back."

Crawford's face changed, the cold, hard anger going out of it. He stared first at the girl, then at the flour stains on Targay's trousers. Then he looked at Mary Olsen and gasped:

"You mean——you mean——?"

Mary chuckled, she knew the danger was passed now and a new life was open to Jack Targay.

"Yes, Joe. Meet Jack Targay, my new cook."

Crawford spun round to face his hands, the anger he'd shown Targay now sent on to them doubled.

"What the hell are you bunch doing?" he roared. "Coming into town and getting booze-blind, then causing trouble for hard-working folks. You just wait till I get you back to the spread. I'll have you on the blister end of a shovel for so long you'll have to learn to ride afresh when I let you finish." He turned to Jack Targay, face beaming with admiration and friendship. "I'm real sorry I called you down like that, friend. Say, about them flapjacks?"

"I'll have them for you soon as I get the flour from Miz Mary's to the kitchen."

"Hank, Billy. Get that sack and tote it down for Jack here. We can't have the best damned cook in the territory straining hisself doing things like that."

The crowd started to disperse now. Dingley glared at the three lawmen, his face still red with anger.

"I'll see this is reported to Captain Mosehan," he snapped.

"When you write to him," Waco's voice was hard under the drawl, "see you tell him it was you let Dancer know when the money was being handed on. And that he had to pull the raid today."

"Me?" Dingley looked as if he would have a stroke. "How dare you imply——"

"Not in so many words you didn't. But you told him. Why do you think he acted so eager to buy that beat-up old ranch when he could pick up a decent place for the same price. He knew you'd be so damned willing to sell it to him that you'd take him out to look it over any day except one. The day you handed the money back to the Army. Cap'n Mosehan didn't tell us what day the money was handed over, he didn't get told it. I guessed it from what you told Dancer."

"Talked to my deputy, he says that you'd pointed Dancer out and told him what a real nice feller Dancer was. Then when Dancer came and said you'd sent him to wait for you the deputy let him in."

Dingley didn't wait to hear any more, he turned and stamped away after the others. Catching up with Targay he slapped the man on the back and offered him a cigar.

Monk walked off to attend to the prisoners and Waco listened to Doc humming a tune as they watched the men walking with Targay and talking with him. Then Waco recognized the tune, he'd heard the Ysabel Kid croon it as he rode circle on a sleeping herd of cattle:

> "Now a mean-looking man is lonely,
> A mean-looking man has no friends,
> When there's trouble in town and he's around,
> They all blame a mean-looking man."

"Who's going to tell Cap'n Bert?" Doc asked.

"Whichever of us, we'll still be hoorawed for a month over this," Waco replied. "You know something, Doc?" he jerked his hand to the men walking with Targay back to the Eating House. "They don't think that mean-looking man's so mean any more."

CASE FOUR

Jase Holmes' Killer

Captain Bertram Mosehan read the telegraph message through once more, whistling tunelessly as he did so. Then taking up a sheaf of wanted posters he riffled through them until he found the one he wanted. Jase Holmes, train robber, gunman and killer was headed this way from a triple killing in Salt Lake City. From the date of the killings he would soon be in Arizona territory, headed for the Mexican border.

Mosehan was making one of his rare visits to Ranger Headquarters in Tucson and was urgently needed down in Cochise County, so there was no chance of going to hunt for Holmes himself. Crossing to the big wall map of the Arizona territory he ran his finger over the paper, following the route Holmes would most likely use. The finger stopped on the town of Garret, up on the edge of the Painted Desert. From there it tracked down to the edge of the Grand Canyon, and the town of Backsight.

Crossing to the desk Mosehan took up a telegraph message form and wrote a short, terse message on it.

"Waco. Leroy. Jase Holmes coming into territory. Head him off at Garret. GET HIM."

The wires sang. Up in Backsight Waco and Doc Leroy threw saddles on their horses, loaded their bedrolls on a packhorse and rode out, headed north.

Night was falling when the two Rangers rode into Garret City and headed into the livery barn. They'd been two days in the saddle and both were now trail dirty and unshaven, hard-looking as a couple of starving razor-back hogs.

"Best see Ben Shields first," Waco suggested. "He might know something."

Doc agreed with this. They knew the town of Garret and were known here from the days when they rode with the Hashknife Outfit.

"Might at that. He'll likely know if Holmes has passed through this way. If he has got through we'll have us a pious time finding him."

Swinging down from their saddles they attended to their horses, neither paying any attention to the old owner of the livery barn as he came from the stable. For his part he saw nothing but the gunhung backs of a pair of Texas cowhands.

"Huh!" the old-timer spat his disgust into the dirt floor. "Two more of you."

Waco turned at the words and found the old-timer eyeing him belligerently. "Cap'n Bert send up more men?"

The old-timer came in closer, peering suspiciously at Waco. Then his face split in a welcoming grin.

"Sorry boy, didn't recognize you. My eyes ain't as good as they used to be."

"Fact being they never were," Waco replied. "Who alls here that we're two more of?"

The owner of the livery barn spat with even more vigour at the wheel of a buggy before answering. "Just about every damned fool, gun-wild kid in the territory."

Waco and Doc stood silent for a moment then looked at each other. "Would it be out of line if I asked why?" Doc inquired.

"They're after the man who killed Jase Holmes."

"Jase Holmes, the owlhoot?" Waco asked.

"How many more Jase Holmes do you know?"

"How'd he die?" Doc ignored the sarcasm in the oldster's voice.

"Took to stealing Whitey Basefield's stud hoss and died of it."

"Nice for Mr. Basefield," Waco remarked dryly.

Neither Doc nor Waco needed any help to add up the prairie sum of that statement. They knew that every trigger-fast young fool in the territory would be flocking in towards Garret with one idea in mind. Find out how fast Jase Holmes' killer was with a gun.

It often surprised and amazed an Eastern dude how news could travel across the range country by the prairie telegraph, bringing men swarming into a town where something was going to happen. It was neither amazing nor strange to Waco and Doc Leroy, for they'd seen it happen too many times. They also knew the end product in this case and what that would mean.

The old-timer watered and grained three stalls and after the horses were inside, helped tote the two young men's gear into his office. He did not express any wonder that they were so far from the Hashknife spread or that they should have arrived in Garret at this moment. Strangely, it never even occurred to him that they might be here looking for Jase Holmes' killer, like the other young men who'd been arriving every day since the shooting.

"Any fool kid who tries his games with them two'll surely wish he hadn't," he said to the big paint stallion Waco rode, as he passed its stall. "Yes, sir, they sure will."

Waco and Doc headed for the Marshal's office, walking along the main street of the town and hearing plenty of noise from the three saloons. Entering the jail they found the Town Marshal, Ben Shields. He sat at his desk, watching the local doctor patch up a young man's shoulder. Three more hard-faced young men were sitting glowering through the bars of the cells.

Shields came to his feet, a tall, powerful-looking man in his early thirties. He was dressed in range clothes and belted a low-tied gun. There was a frank and open friendliness about him which was offset by the grim set of his jaw and something in his eyes. Waco studied him, knowing Shields as a square lawman and a brave one. That look in his eyes wasn't fear but it was something near to it.

"Howdy you pair," Shields greeted. "What're you doing in town?"

"Cap'n Mosehan sent us up here. Thought we might be able to pick up Jase Holmes," Doc replied. "Only it looks like we came too late."

"Four days too late." There was a brittle harshness in Shields' tones.

The doctor finished bandaging up the man's wounded shoulder and growled, "I've got to go out to the Brant place to deliver a baby. If any more of them take lead let 'em bleed to death."

Shields shoved the wounded man into the cell and locked the door as the doctor stamped off into the night. Then Shields came back to the desk and looked at Waco and Doc, an unspoken question in his eyes.

"How'd that happen?" Waco asked.

"Just one of the shootings, that's all." Shields' voice was showing strain. "We've had three killed and two bad wounded besides these bunch."

"Sounds worse than Dodge City when ole Clay Allison used to come in," Doc said sympathetically. "All of them after Mr. Basefield?"

"Every last one."

"How'd it happen?" Waco inquired.

"Holmes came in afork a half-dead hoss. He saw Whitey Basefield's stud hoss at the rail of the Bell Saloon and thought to take it. Whitey came out just as Holmes was untying the reins. They drew and Holmes died."

"Said Whitey being a fast gun?" Doc inquired.

"That's the hell of it. Whitey ain't but average with a gun at best. I've got Holmes' gear here. Checked the holster, inside was roughed up."

Neither Waco nor Doc needed to be told any more than that. They were skilled and practised handlers of guns and knew all too well what a roughened holster meant. In a draw and shoot affair where a draw which took up a second was called slow, split seconds counted. That vital speed the smooth inside of a holster gave was important. The loss of it due to the roughening of the leather, was enough to cost a man his life. One mistake was fatal. Jase Holmes had made that one mistake.

"Bad thing to happen," Waco remarked, his voice soft and gentle. "Man doesn't have it happen more than once."

"Amen!" Doc agreed.

Shields shook his head as if to clear it, then he glanced at the two young Texans whom he'd known as cowhands for the Hashknife.

"You boys doing anything?"

"Not now. Like I said, Cap'n. Bert sent us along to try

and take Holmes. He's wanted bad in Salt Lake City," Waco explained.

For a moment Shields was puzzled, then he remembered hearing about Bertram Mosehan starting the Arizona Rangers. He could guess that Mosehan would take this pair of hell-twisters along with him.

"How'd so many of these guns get here in this time?" Doc asked.

"Was some trouble up Fredonia way. Looked like a war starting up. But it was stopped by a couple of your boys. The guns came on down here with their pay in their pockets and time on their hands."

From outside they heard the thunder of shots and all looked at each other. Shields knew without asking that they would help him. Some of the tense tightness left him. He picked up his hat and walked towards the door, the other two following him out.

After they'd brought back the wounded survivor of the shooting scrape and Doc patched him up prior to shoving him in the cells, the three lawmen gathered at the desk. Neither Doc nor Waco realized how many men there were in town, all waiting for a crack at Jase Holmes' killer. They were in the saloons, on the sidewalk, all young men, all wearing guns and all with the same idea in mind. Meet and beat the man who killed Jase Holmes.

"How much longer is this going to last?" he asked bitterly. "I can't handle them much longer and I can't get a deputy now."

Waco watched the marshal, knowing it wasn't entirely, or even partly, fear that made him like this. It was the constant living with a gun, living on his nerves and waiting for his town to blow wide open. It was the constant alertness and the sense of futility. That was making Ben Shields like this. Other lawmen had gone the same way under similar circumstances. Wild Bill Hickok went that way the day he was in a gunfight and heard someone running behind him. He'd turned and shot, killing a friend who was coming to help him.

Ben Shields was going that same way and he needed help about as bad as a man could need it.

"Where at's this gent Basefield?" Waco asked.

"Out at his spread. I sent word for him to stay there until this blows over. His foreman wanted to bring the ranch crew in and clear the town. I stopped him. I didn't want a full-out war on my hands. Tad Bowmain, him being Whitey's foreman, ain't the sort to play games."

"We know ole Tad," Doc put in. "Waco rode with him in CA and I met him when he came down to the Hashknife."

"Waal, he's holding the hands back, at a spread. They're primed for war though. Couple of guns got real smart, they went out to the Basefield spread to hunt Whitey up. They came back to town on a rail."

"Knowing ole Tad they were real lucky to come back at all," Waco replied, looking out of the window. Three more gun-hung young men rode past, headed for one of the saloons.

It was then Waco knew he must carry out his plan. It was a plan based on his knowledge of gunmen. He knew how they reacted and what made them tick. He also knew the only way to handle the matter. The wanted, every one of them, to be the man who faced down Jase Holmes' killer. They wanted the reputation of being the man who killed the man who was faster than Jase Holmes.

Under normal circumstances it would have been more difficult, for the men would not have congregated this fast. However, there had been a range war brewing near Fredonia and both sides hired an army of fighting men. Pete

Glendon and Billy Speed, two Rangers, had arrived to end the trouble. The gunhands, paid off and with no hope of further employment, would have drifted off, scattering in search of other work. When word reached them of the killing of Jase Holmes they came to Garret to see if they could match shots with the man who killed him.

"You got something on your mind, boy?" Shields asked hopefully.

"Sure." Waco dropped his voice so the men in the cells could not hear him. "Come sunup me'n ole Doc are headed for Basefield's place."

Doc Leroy had long since decided his wild, reckless young partner could not say or do anything which would surprise him again. He found he was wrong. Shields listened to Waco's plan with fascinated disbelief. It gave him a feeling he'd only known once before. That was when he was laid up in some thick brush with three bronco Apaches looking to take his head home with them as a gift to their girl friends.

Letting out his breath in a long slow gasp he asked, "Have you thought what it'll mean to you?"

"Sure, reckon I have. Anyways, the way ole Cap'n Bert keeps us on the move they won't never have time to catch up on ole Doc and me. And if they do, time they get to where we are we'll have left for some other place."

The following morning at sunup Waco and Doc rode out of the town, following Shields' directions for finding the Basefield Ranch. Doc watched his partner as they left the town behind them. For a time he was silent, then finally he said:

"You're loco, boy."

"Reckon I am."

"Waal, the worst that can happen is that we'll have to

down a couple of them afore we leave here."

"Sure," Waco agreed. "That's the worst that could happen."

A man rode into Garret by the south trail about the same time the two Rangers left by the north. He left his powerful roan stallion in the livery barn and strode out on the street, a tall, powerful man, his handsome, cultured face at odds with his sober-coloured range clothes and the low-tied brace of matched Colt Civilian Peacemakers. Striding along the street with a leisurely, contemptuous stride, looking neither right nor left, he headed for the first of the three saloons. Pushing open the batwing doors he stepped in, cold contempt in his eyes as he looked around at the gunmen. Silence fell over the room and all eyes were on him as he spoke, his voice a gentle, cultured deep south drawl.

"Gentlemen, the name is Ringo, Johnny Ringo to my less cultured friends. Any man who aims to face Whitey Basefield will have to get me first."

Unaware of this new development Waco and Doc rode along the wagon trail to the Basefield Ranch. Although neither were used to this section, their previous business near Garret having been on the other side of town, they expected no difficulty in finding their way to the ranch. Long experience of crossing the open range country gave them the ability to do so with only the briefest directions.

The ranch lay some five miles from town and when they could see it in the distance they allowed their horses to make better time. Neither gave any attention to a small *bosque* of cottonwood trees some thirty yards to the right of the rail trail they were following.

The rifle shot hit the ground ahead of them and sang into the air with the vicious sobbing whine of a ricochet. From the *bosque* a voice yelled:

"Sit fast. We could have downed you just as well as missing, had we wanted."

Three young cowhands rode out of the cottonwood trees, each one with a rifle on his knees. Waco tensed, then relaxed again, for these were no gunhands, proddy killers looking to make a reputation. They were cowhands and he could see Tad Bowmain's training in the way they handled themselves.

Fanning out, with their rifles held ready for use, the three young men closed in on Waco and Doc. The centre rider was their leader apparently, a freckle-faced young hand who should have been smiling, but was grim and determined-looking. He scowled at the two Texans and asked:

"Didn't them last two teach you nothing?"

"Sure, but we come just the same," Doc replied. "Wouldn't do no good to tell you that you're making a mistake."

"Nope, it wouldn't. The only mistake round here is you two," the stocky young hand at the right growled. "We should burn you right now and leave you for the other buzzards."

"Hold it, Beck," the other one who'd spoken first put in. "Ole Tad, he told us if we found any more of them to take them in so he could handle them."

Waco sat still and allowed the young men to take his guns. The trio were well enough trained to make any attempt at objection dangerous, even for a pair of men as fast in action as Waco and Doc.

Shoving the matched staghorn-butted Artillery Peacemakers into his waistband, the leader of the trio snapped, "Head for the house. Try and light out if you want to. I'd surely admire to see you try and outrun a bullet."

Waco and Doc rode in silence under the guns of their

captors. Doc was wishing that the Rangers wore their badges in plain view, for he did not like seeing his ivory-butted Colt Civilian Peacemaker sticking in the waistband of the young man called Beck. Both noticed the cowhands were cautious and far from being gun-wild. But they were silent and the cowhand was not by nature silent, when one was it could be an ominous sign. Waco hoped that Bowmain was at the spread and not out on the range, otherwise there might be bad trouble.

They rode down towards the ranch and from the cook-shack came four more tough, handy-looking young men. For a moment Waco felt uneasy, for Tad Bowmain was not with them. Then from the ranch house, along with a tall, handsome young man and a very pretty blonde woman, came the stocky, craggy shape of Tad Bowmain, late puncher for Mr. Clayton Allison, of the Washita River, Texas.

"What's all this, Danny?" Bowmain asked, although he was grinning as he looked the prisoners over.

"Couple more guns coming after Whitey," the young hand with Waco's guns replied. "Brung them in so's you can tromp some sense into them."

"Real good idea, though it'd take a mite of doing," Bowmain agreed. Then, "Do you know who they are?"

"Don't know, or care."

"Best take a look at the backstrap of one of them Colt guns."

Dan lifted the Colt from his waistband, turning it and looking down at the inscription on the blued backstrap. His face went through a series of changes as he read it aloud.

"For our pard, Waco. From Ole Devil's Floating Out-fit." Then to Bowmain, who was studying them all with mocking eyes. "You mean this here's—"

"Sure," Bowmain agreed as the words trailed off. "Waco and Doc Leroy."

Waco and Doc sat back, grinning at the consternation the discovery of their identity was causing. Bowmain chuckled and asked, "Bert Mosehan got round to firing you at last?"

"Could call it that," Waco answered. "When he formed the Rangers he took me'n Doc along with him. Say now, Dan, how's about giving me my guns back. You've played with them for long enough."

Dan handed over the guns but first, replying, "Shucks, take the fool things, I've got a good'n. Anyways, it wasn't my idea to take them. I'm too young, too sweet, too——"

"Smelly 'n' ornery," Beck finished for his pard, offering Doc's gun back to its owner. "Here Doc. Don't you go letting no more big boys take it from you."

Doc couldn't think of an adequate answer for this remark so he took the gun, dusted it off with great care, drew the hammer to half cock and rolled the cylinder as if he thought Beck might have helped himself to the ammunition. Then he holstered the gun and looked at Bowmain.

"Way you carry on when folks come visiting a man'd say you've got some real close borrowing neighbours."

They swung down from their horses at Bowmain's invitation and were introduced to Whitey Basefield and his wife. Waco took a liking to the rancher from the start. Whitey was a friendly looking man, certainly not a proddy gun-fighting killer. His wife was pretty and Waco guessed she loved Whitey very much, there were lines under her eyes that told of worry about his present troubles. They made such a nice-looking couple that he was more determined than ever to help them out.

They shook hands, then Waco got down to business. With Holmes dead he wanted to get back to make his report to Mosehan and allow the Ranger Captain to call "Keno" on this mission.

"Like to see you, Whitey, happen these tough hands o' your'n will let me," he said. "I'll promise not to shoot you in the leg until after sundown."

"Sure, come on into the house and take a bite to eat. I reckon the boys will trust you that far."

The Basefields ushered their guests and Bowmain into the house and Whitey led the way into a clean and tidy sittingroom. Mrs. Basefield looked these two young Texas men over and, like her husband and Bowmain, wondered what brought them here. She remembered hearing their names mentioned by Bowmain several times when the hands were discussing gunfighters. She also remembered that those two names, Waco and Doc Leroy were placed among the top men like Dusty Fog, Mark Counter, Wes Hardin or Bill Longley. Since the killing of Jase Holmes, Sheila Basefield had lived in fear of men like those and now two were here at the ranch.

"You've heard what's happening in town?" Waco got right down to cases.

Basefield nodded, "We've heard."

"Comes the end of the roundup we'll likely head for town and have us a clean-out day," Bowmain went on.

"There isn't that much time to spare," Waco replied. "Tomorrow I want you and Whitey to come into town with me'n Doc."

Sheila Basefield was at the table, filling glasses with milk. She gave a little cry, and dropped one, which shattered on the floor at her feet, but she did not look down. Catching her husband's arm she looked at Waco and gasped, "What do you mean?"

"Like this, ma'am," Doc said. "The town is swarming with guns all itching to get a crack at Jase Holmes' killer.

Waco's just aiming to give them a fresh mark to go for."

Of the three inquiring faces which turned to Waco, perhaps only Bowmain had any idea what lay behind those casual words, and even he could not believe any man would take such a chance.

Waco's next words proved that Bowmain was wrong, for there was a man willing to take the chance.

"I want to draw against you and beat you to the shot."

Whitey stared without speaking, hardly believing his ears. His wife clutched at his arm and held on to it. The words were spoken with no more emotion than had they been a casual remark against the weather. For a moment Mrs. Basefield thought of running to fetch the crew, but her husband restrained her.

"You'd best explain that, Waco," he said softly.

"Just come out back for a minute first," Waco replied. "I want to prove something to you."

Basefield looked at Bowmain and his foreman nodded. Still confused, the rancher followed Waco and Doc from the room and out to the rear of the house. Bowmain gave Sheila what should have been a reassuring smile, but which was more like the grin of a skull, then followed the men out.

From his pocket, Doc took a dollar and walked about ten feet from Waco, then held out his right arm with the coin between his thumb and forefinger. For an instant he stood like that.

Waco's right hand dipped faster than the eye could follow.

The fingers curled round the butt of his gun while the thumb eared back the hammer even as the gun was lifting out of the holster. Held hip high, in the centre of Waco's body, the gun crashed and the coin was torn from Doc's fingers.

Whitey Basefield gulped. He'd thought his foreman was fast with a gun, but this did not stop at just being fast. He licked his lips, then as his ranch hands came charging around the corner with guns out, he said, "Well?"

"Just wanted to prove to you that I can hit my mark," Waco answered.

Bowmain told the hands to go back and finish their twice interrupted meal. He knew what Waco had in mind and knew why the Texan was doing it. Then he followed the Basefields and the two Rangers back into the house again.

"What do you want to do?" Whitey asked, knowing the display he'd just seen was not the mere action of a man showing off his prowess with a gun.

"Depends on you. Happen you'll let me, I'll shoot your gun clear out of your hand. Worse that'll happen is the bullet'll sprain your wrist, or the lead'll dust your hand."

"What good will that do?" Sheila asked. "And if it will do any, why must you do it in town. Can't you do it here?"

"No, ma'am, I can't."

"Why not?" She still stared with fascinated attention at Doc Leroy, wondering how any man could calmly take such a risk. Standing there holding a coin in his right hand——. His right hand. She looked at the butt of his gun holstered at his right side. A man must have a lot of faith in his friend to take such a risk with his gun hand.

"Because there are none of the gunhands here to see it," Waco replied. "I want to prove to them that Whitey isn't a fast gun. They aren't after Whitey, because they're friends of Jase Holmes or for any personal reason. They just want, every one of them, to be able to say he stacked against the man who was faster than Jase Holmes."

"Well?" Sheila could still not follow Waco's reasoning.

"If Whitey is beat to the shot there's nothing to be gained in going after him."

"Oh!" She looked at Bowmain, who nodded in agreement. Then she saw something more, something her husband and Bowmain both knew. "But then they'll be after you."

"Shucks, ma'am. I never thought of that." Waco's voice was mild and innocent. " 'Sides I've got ole Doc here to protect me."

Whitey shook his head. "I can't ask any man to do that for me."

"You didn't ask me, I'm telling you. It's the only way." Waco's voice had changed now and become hard and incisive. "Mister, that town's fuller of guns than fleas on an Apache dawg. They're going to stay on until one of them gets a crack at you. They've got money, but when it runs out they won't be caring how they get more. And another thing, those would-be Wes Hardins have only fought among themselves so far but sooner or later some innocent gent is going to get killed."

"We could take the boys in and clear the town," Bowmain growled.

"Sure and get a lot of your boys killed off," Waco answered. "They're good boys, but they're not professional guns like that bunch in town. Besides, if you win you'll have a name for being a hard crew and you know what that means, Tad. You rode with one."

Bowmain nodded. He'd ridden with Clay Allison long enough to know what it meant, having that reputation. It meant that every other ranch crew would set themselves out to see how true the reputation was. Law in towns the crew went near would be suspicious and sooner or later it would come to killing again.

"There's more than that to it," Doc put in seriously,

looking at Sheila Basefield. "Whitey killed a man who needed killing. A man who was set to kill him. That man was known to be very fast with a gun. Sure, I know Holmes' gun stuck as he was drawing, but those guns in town don't know it. So unless this thing's proved and proved real fast there'll be some gun-trying for him. Then Whitey's going to have to kill again and again until one of them beats him."

"They're right, honey," Whitey said, his voice hard. "I'm riding into town and doing what Waco wants."

The afternoon was drawing to a close when Waco rode alone into Garret and halted the borrowed horse in front of the Marshal's office. He swung down and watched Doc Leroy, Basefield and Bowmain coming from the livery barn where they had just put up the horses, including Waco's big paint stallion. They walked towards the Silver Dollar Saloon and Waco was about to follow them when Ben Shields came to the door of his office, looking worried.

"You've got to call it off, boy," he said. "Johnny Ringo's in town and he says he wants first crack at Whitey."

"Then he'll just be disappointed," Waco replied, setting his guns right as he walked off towards the Silver Dollar.

Striding along the street Waco turned Shields' words over in his mind. He knew Johnny Ringo's reputation of being a man of his word. Yet never before, as far as Waco knew, had Ringo hunted a man just for the sake of a reputation shoot-out. It was mostly the other way round, would-be killers and hard men sought out the heads of the Galeyville rustlers to try out their gunspeed against. Ringo, co-ruler of the Galeyville bunch and his partner, Curly Bill Brocious, were not the sort to waste valuable time that could be spent gambling or drinking in pursuing profitless shooting scrapes.

Not that Ringo or Brocious were scared of matching shots with any man. Fast and deadly with his guns, Johnny Ringo was scared of nothing. He was one man who Wyatt Earp and the rest of Tombstone "Law and Order" crowd steered clear of and wanted no doings with; in fact, on one occasion Ringo made all those stalwart defenders of "Law and Order" hunt for their holes.

One thing Waco was sure of was that Ringo would not take kindly to this flouting of his orders.

The batwings opened at Waco's push and he entered, halting just inside to look around him. There were about ten young gunmen hanging around the saloon, all watching the trio at the bar. Apart from them and the bardog the place was empty and silent.

Waco crossed the room and halted, facing Whitey Basefield. In a voice which carried to every man in the room he said:

"You're Whitey Basefield, the man who downed Jase Holmes. Way I hear it Holmes let the inside of his holster rough up. Mister, you were some lucky."

One of the gunmen, half drunk, lurched to his feet and came alongside Waco, hand hovering the butt of his gun.

"That's what I heard, too, and I aim——"

Waco pivoted round on his toes, his right hand gun coming out and making a dully flashing arc under the lights of the bar. It smashed down on to the young man's head, dropping him to the ground. In a continuation of the same move Waco brought the gun round to cover the other men. They sat very still, every one of the hard-faced young gunmen. Every one of them thought he was fast with a gun but this soft talking Texas boy did not stop just at being fast.

"Basefield's my meat," Waco said softly. "I'll kill the next man who tries to cut in."

Whitey could hardly believe the change which had come over Waco. He'd known killers and fast gunmen before, men who lived by the speed of their draw and were masters of their trade. This was one who stood before him now. A fast draw fighting man reared on the cattle trails of Texas, brought to full prominence riding for Ole Devil Hardin's floating outfit, matured in the Ranger service. Jase Holmes had been in that same class with a gun, it was only the mischance of his holster having roughened up that kept Whitey Basefield alive.

"What do you want?" Whitey could hardly recognize his own voice, so distorted by strain it sounded.

"I want you to draw!"

Looking past Waco, Basefield was reminded of a fight he'd once seen between two wolves. The other members of the pack sat just like those gunmen, watching with savage eyes to see which would win.

Whitey Basefield's hand dropped towards his gun. Every man here could see that this was not the flickering, sight defying move of a chain-lightning killer. His hand was closing on the gun and lifting it before Waco made his move. The Texan's hands went down like the flickering tongue of a snake. The matched guns were out of their holsters and the right roared, throwing lead at Basefield.

Whitey felt as if his arms had been struck by a club, the gun was torn from his grasp even as it came from leather. His hand and arm were driven back into the bar with numbing force and he stood there, sweat pouring down his face.

Without even another look at Whitey, Waco came round and faced the crowd, his guns still in his hands.

"Does that answer your question?" he asked.

There the crowd had it laid flat before them. If any man wanted to take up the challenge, all he had to do was say the word and he would be accommodated. Slowly the young gunmen turned back to their games or their drinking. For the moment not one of them would take a chance. They'd seen Whitey draw and knew he was no fast killer and that the Texan's words must be true. Later some of them might feel like taking him up, but not just now.

Doc Leroy and Bowmain helped Whitey Basefield into the back room, for he was suffering from the unpleasant shock of having a bullet come so close to him. Also, as Waco guessed, the bullet sprained his wrist, but that was nothing and would be over in a few days.

Two of the gunmen slipped from the saloon. Waco watched them go, knowing they would be headed round the saloons telling of how Jase Holmes' killer failed. It was only a matter of time before Johnny Ringo heard the word and came to see the rash man who went against his word.

Five minutes ticked by. The bardog polished his glasses with one frightened eye on the door. Then his face went pale and carefully he lowered the glass he was polishing to the counter and a grin came to his face, a very weak grin, like a man joking with the executioner.

"Evening, Mr. Ringo," he said.

Johnny Ringo let the swinging doors of the saloon close behind him and stood just as Waco stood when he first entered. Ringo's eyes went slowly round the room, then came to rest on Waco, recognizing him as the only one present who would be worthy of his skill. Moving forward he halted six feet from Waco.

"Are you the man who shot Whitey Basefield?"

"Sure."

"You heard the word I put out?"

"I heard."

"And you still went ahead and drew against him. I wouldn't think you were that kind." Ringo's cultured, deep south drawl matched Waco's Texas accent, neither speaking in loud tones, yet their every word carrying to the watchers.

"Man does what he has to do," Waco answered.

Ringo nodded, wondering why this tall young Texas man, obviously one of the real fast men, would waste time going in for reputation shootings.

"You called it right. I said I'd kill the man who shot Whitey Basefield and I never break my word."

Neither moved. They stood there, tense, yet relaxed, alert, yet not obviously so. There was death in the air, death from the guns of those two men standing at the bar.

Not one of the watchers lifted their voices to more than a sigh, even the half-drunks were cold sober now. They watched and waited, wondering which of these two, if either, would be on his feet when the smoke cleared.

The door of the backroom opened and Whitey Basefield came out, stopped and took in the scene, then came forward until he stood between the two.

"What the hell?" he asked. "Waco, Johnny, stop it and get the place cleared."

Ringo relaxed slightly, looking first at Basefield, then at Waco. He turned his back on Waco and looked round the room, the contempt in his eyes again as he studied the gunmen.

"Gentlemen, the last man through the door incurs my serious displeasure. Drift and *pronto*."

There was a sudden concerted rush for the door. Every man amongst the gunmen knew that never was Johnny Ringo more dangerous than when that mockingly polite way of talking was in use. In later years, hard-wintering at the slack times the bardog would insist that his bar cleared in half a minute. In actual fact it was four times as long before the batwing doors swung closed behind the last scared-looking gunman.

"What's this all about?" Waco asked, looking at Whitey.

Whitey started to laugh. It was a near hysterical laugh brought on by the tension and this near tragedy so narrowly averted.

"This is a laugh," he said at the end.

"I admire a sense of humour," Doc Leroy growled from the door, where he'd been watching everything.

"Well," Whitey explained, "it's like this. Waco here starts to help me and so does Johnny."

Waco turned to Ringo. "Way I heard it you said you'd down any man who went for Whitey before you tried."

"The trouble with honest citizens is they always misquote me," Ringo answered. "My statement being that I would down the man who faced Whitey."

The doors opened and Ben Shields came in with a ten-gauge under his arm. He went straight up to Ringo and said:

"I'm sorry about this, Johnny. It was me told Waco and got him off wrong."

Ringo threw back his head and roared with laughter. "A lawman apologizing to me. That's the best I've heard."

Waco hitched up his belt and looked at the others, he could see a different light in Ben Shields' eyes.

"It's time this town had a good clearout," he said. "Coming Ben."

Shields hefted the shotgun and nodded, then inspiration hit him. "Need me a good deputy for a spell, Johnny."

"Me a deputy?" he asked, then his dark face split in a smile realizing this was Shields' way of apologizing. "Certainly. Curly Bill has been crowing about how he helped

Beck collect the Cochise County taxes. I'd like to be a
deputy too."

The customers of the Garret City saloon looked up as
the four grim men entered. Waco stepped forward and his
eyes seemed to be picking out every gunman individually.

"I'm the man who beat Jase Holmes' killer. Whitey
Basefield isn't and never was fast with a gun. He beat
Holmes because Holmes let the inside of his holster rough
up. Any man here who wants to take me say the word.
Stand right up and cut loose your wolf."

The men in the saloon sat very still, each waiting for the
next man to make the move. Two slow minutes ticked by
without there being any takers, then Waco went on:

"One hour after dawn tomorrow I'll be coming round
town. I'll take it as real personal if I find any one of you
still here."

"The ones Waco doesn't get will be shared equally between Doc, Ben and myself, gentlemen," Ringo went on.
"More than that, if I ever hear of any damned fool going
after Whitey again I'll find that man and make him wish
he'd been caught by the Apaches."

From the silence Waco knew they'd won and that Jase
Holmes' killer need worry no more.

Statute of Limitations

Sam Strogoff, head of the South-west Section of Pinkerton's Agency, came into Captain Bertram Mosehan's office with all the aggressive air of a small man in a position of authority. His attitude was that of condescension, as if he were here to make Mosehan some great offer, like employment with his agency, not the attitude of a man come to beg favours.

Strogoff looked round the room. It was small, barely furnished and far different from his own sumptuous office. The head of the Arizona Rangers was content to do business here, with only one desk scarred by spur and cigarette, in a bare little room with a large map of the territory on one wall. Not that Mosehan was in the least worried, for he was but rarely in the office at all, spending most of his time in the field.

He was here this morning, seated at one side of his

desk, looking over two young Rangers who were studying a pile of wanted posters. Strogoff glanced at them, saw they were both Texas men, tall and handy looking. He knew them both and his eyes closed in a scowl.

"Howdy Strogoff." There was a lack of warmth in Mosehan's greeting. "What can I do for you?"

"There's a man up at Canvastown our Agency wants bringing in," Strogoff replied, taking out a wanted poster and passing it to Mosehan. "He's wanted on a charge of attempted fraud. Tried to pass a dud cheque at the Chicago First National Bank, they queried the signature and he slugged a guard, then escaped."

"It took you a long time to find him." Mosehan checked the date on the faded and well-worn poster. "The Statute of Limitations runs out in about three weeks."

"That's why we want him."

"Why?" Doc Leroy asked, as he accepted the poster Mosehan held out. "He didn't get away with anything and it looks like the guard didn't die, or the charge would be more than just attempted fraud."

"He broke the law," Strogoff's chest puffed out importantly.

"Hallelujah!" Waco said drily, "and the great Pinkertons never did that themselves, did they?"

Strogoff reached a hand for the poster, his face flushed and angry. "I came here for help, not to get insulted by your hired men, Mosehan. I can get all the smart answers I want from my wife."

"Why didn't the man who located this feller bring him in?" Mosehan asked. "Or are you only guessing he's there."

"One of our operatives saw him. He'd been on the case and remembered the man. Changed his name to Turing now, Ace Turing they call him. Got a scar on the back of his hand. The operative was almost sure he recognized the man, and came back to check on the posters and make sure."

"Turning popular in Canvastown?" Mosehan inquired.

"Some."

"Couldn't be fast with a gun as well?"

"He could be, the operative didn't stop to see. The only law there's a big, dumb, thick constable and he wouldn't be any help against a man like——" Strogoff stopped as he realized he was saying too much.

"So I'm supposed to send my men after some man who's too good with a gun for your operatives," Mosehan growled. "That's good, real good."

Strogoff scowled back at Mosehan. He was used to getting more respect and co-operation from local and civic law.

"I'll report this to Head Office. Here I am, stuck with every operative in the field on the Army payroll robbery. So I come to get help from the Territorial Rangers and what do I get. Smart talk. Do I have to go to the Governor and get him to tell you?"

"You can go to hell for all of me." Mosehan's own temper was rising now. "But when you see Governor Murphy you make good and sure you tell him your man was scared to bring Turing in. The Governor'll be real pleased. He'll be real pleased to know that you want to use the Rangers to help keep your Agency's reputation up."

Strogoff's face flushed red, those words hit home to the mark. There was not much to be gained in taking this man in, except it would be good advertising for the Pinkerton Agency. It would look good on record that after all these years the Pinkertons, alert and unsleeping as always, had located a wanted man and brought him to justice.

"All right, Mosehan," Strogoff hissed. "You damned Rangers think——"

Waco's chair slid back and he came to his feet in a lithe move.

"There's two ways out of this office. The door or the window. Take your choice."

"Choke off, boy!" Mosehan snapped, for he knew Waco was more than capable of throwing Strogoff through one or the other. "We'll fetch him in for you, Strogoff. Otherwise you might hire a bounty hunter and have him brought in dead."

"Say," Waco put in, "seeing as how we're working for Pinkertons now, do we get a bomb to throw through the feller's mother's window? Real Pinkerton style."

Strogoff started forward, his fists clenched, then he stopped for he'd seen too many examples of Waco's fistic ability to want to try his luck. He knew the Texan was ready, willing and more than able to take him apart.

Any mention of bombs tended to make the Pinkerton men act like that since the incident at the home of Jesse James. Pinkertons insisted that they threw a pot of greek fire through the window of the Samuels' place, not a bomb. However, no loyal son of Dixie would ever believe that it was other than a bomb which killed Jesse James' brother and tore his mother's arm off.

"I'll not forget you, Texas man," he snarled.

"Waco gets you like that," Doc put in. "He's cute."

"We'll bring Turing in for you, Strogoff," Mosehan's words cut in to prevent any more trouble. "Leave the warrant and the poster, then move on. I'm busy."

Strogoff tossed the wanted poster and warrant on to the desk top, looked around the bare room again, walked towards the door, halted and turned.

"He goes under the name of Ace Turing, like I said.

Owns and runs a saloon and gaming house. You'll find him——!"

"When we need lessons I'll let you know," Mosehan barked.

Without another word Strogoff turned and walked out of the room, slamming the door behind him. For a long time Mosehan sat looking at the two papers on the desk, then up at Waco and Doc. He pushed the two papers round with the tip of his finger, whistling tunelessly. At last he made his decision.

"Go up and bring him in."

Anger showed in Waco's blue eyes. He growled, "I likes doing Pinkerton's dirty work for them, I do."

"Sure, makes a man feel real good inside," Doc Leroy agreed, but he took up the two papers and passed them to his partner. "It'll take us near on a week to get to Canvastown."

Mosehan watched the two young men set their hats right, then walk towards the door. He did not speak until they were about to go out through it.

"Waco, Doc!" They stopped and looked back. "Don't bust a gut trying to get him."

Five days later Waco and Doc rode towards the tent-built community of Canvastown. They stopped their horses and looked down at the straggling mass of tents in the curve of a small river. Facing the largest of these canvas structures a large, wooden building was being erected. It looked nearly completed and although they could not tell from such a distance, Waco and Doc would have taken bets it was a saloon.

Doc pulled at the lead-rope of the pack-pony as they started forward towards the town. Waco stopped for another moment, watched the deserted streets and a frown came to his face.

"Where's everybody at?" he asked.

"You expecting maybe a brass band and the City Fathers waiting to greet us?" Doc replied, although he, too, was unable to see why the streets should be so deserted at this hour of the day.

Even as they rode into town they heard the sounds which came from the big canvas structure facing the wooden building. They wondered if a fight was going on, for screams, yells, cheers, thuds and crashes sounded. Even as Waco and Doc watched, the sidewall of the tent bulged, jerked and then ripped open. Two screaming, fighting women catapulted out, clinging to each other, then rolled over and over, tearing at hair, clawing and battling like a pair of enraged wildcats.

The taller of the pair was a shapely blonde and even mussed up as she was now, showed signs of being something of a beauty. Her expensive green, satin frock was in tatters, her black stockings torn and she had lost one shoe. From her dress, she was a worker in a saloon.

The other woman was not so tall, but heavier built. From her torn old gingham dress, bare legs and cheap shoes she wore, she was not another of the saloon clan, but one of the poorer townswomen. She was a flaming red-headed woman, ruddy cheeked and would have been pleasant-looking if her face wasn't twisted in an expression of rage.

Fights between dance-hall girls were not uncommon, but only very rarely did the good women of the towns go near the painted workers. Certainly they would never pick a fight with one. However, Waco and Doc were not going to interfere, they were not going to get involved in a thing like that if they could help it.

From the torn wall of the building, making it larger all the time, came a crowd of excited, shouting, cheering people. Yet it was a mixed crowd, for not only were the saloon girls represented, but there were women who by their dress should not have been in a saloon at all.

From the way the two fighting women were now staggering about it was obvious they'd put up quite a fight inside. They were back on their feet again, but struggling, gasping and sobbing in the last stages of exhaustion. The blonde swung a wild punch; it came round with her swinging body's weight behind it and the red-head walked right into it, jaw first. From the way she went down, arms thrown wide and limp, Waco saw she wouldn't be getting up for a spell.

The blonde's knees buckled up under her and she went down on to her face by the side of the red-head.

Instantly a thin-faced woman dressed in a sober black frock, lunged forward, her face savage, as she screamed:

"Now let's run the rest of the hussies out of town."

The dance-hall girls gathered in a protective group, ready to defend their friend. The blonde was trying to push herself up on her hands, but was unable, and subsided with a groan. Then the thin-faced woman jumped forward and drew back her foot. A big, smiling, red-faced man, who could not have been anything but Irish from the look of him, pushed forward and pulled the woman back.

"All right now, me darlin's," he said. "That's all, git on home wid yez. You was all going to do so much in there, but when it come to the time, sure there wasn't but my Mary who'd face up to Miz Libby. Now home wid yez and we'll see what me wife says, when she can."

The crowd halted uncertainly, but the thin-faced woman was not going to give up that easily. She turned to a big, sullen-looking man standing next to her and looking undecided what to do.

"Are you going to stand for that?" she screamed. "Harcourt, Paddy Ryan pushed me. Do something!"

The crowd was getting ugly. They were motivated by the desire to protect the woman. At any other time they would have regarded Mrs. Harcourt as a pious, sanctimonious nuisance, but right now she was the down-trodden heroine of right and virtue. They crowded forward, towards the big Irishman, waving their fists and shouting.

Waco's right-hand gun crashed into the air. He kicked his heels into the flanks of the seventeen-hand paint horse, causing it to leap forward at the crowd. The people scattered as they saw the huge, savage-looking stallion coming at them, ridden by a hard-faced Texas boy. They scattered and one man, trying to impress someone, lunged forward, grabbing at Waco's boot. The pistol rose and fell on the man's head, dropping him to the ground.

"Rangers here!" Waco snapped, over the blued barrels of his matched Colt Artillery Peacemakers. "Break it up, all of you!"

The crowd halted. In the time they'd been operating the Arizona Rangers had built themselves quite a reputation. These two young men on their horses and facing the crowd were alike in some ways. The faces, one tanned, handsome and intelligent, the other palled, studious and almost mild looking, were alike in their lack of fear, or any sign of indecision. Not one of the men in that crowd doubted that here were two Territorial Rangers, even though they did not wear any badge.

The crowd backed off slightly and Doc holstered his Colt, then swung down from his big black stallion. He saw a woman hurrying along the street towards the crowd and thought nothing of it, she would be coming to see what was going on here.

Bending over the red-head he moved her head gently,

then glanced at the blood which ran from her nose and the split lip.

"What's the game, Ranger?" Ryan asked suspiciously, as Doc tore a piece of the red-head's dress off to wipe away the blood.

"If those two ladies are hurt bad they'll likely need some help," Doc answered. He rolled the blonde on to her back gently and examined her, ignoring the hostile glances of the crowd. "Looks a mite bruised and scratched up, likely your lady there'll not feel like chewing steak for a spell, but there's nothing real serious that I can see. They're just plain tuckered out."

"And why shouldn't they be?" Ryan growled, studying the slim young Ranger who talked like he knew what he was doing. "After fifteen minutes of the finest, roughest, toughest, knockdown, stamp-on and drag-out fight it's ever been me pleasure to watch. Would you be a doctor then?"

"I know a mite about it," Doc replied.

The woman who'd been running along the street forced her way through the crowd. She was blonde, slight and still pretty. But her face showed worry.

"Did you say there was a doctor here, Paddy?" she asked. "Thank God for that. Doctor, will you come with me?"

"I'm not a regular doctor ma'am," Doc replied. He'd attended medical school, but did not finish the course. However, on the cattle trails, Doc Leroy gained a reputation of being able to handle anything from pulling a tooth and setting a broken bone to producing a baby and removing an appendix.

The woman gave no sign of having heard him. She gripped his arm and looked at him, "Please, doctor, come and look at my little boy. He's got such terrible pains in his stomach and sweat's pouring out of him. He's in agony, doctor."

Doc looked at Waco and the young Ranger could see his friend was very worried. He nodded and Doc reached for the reins of his big black. In the saddle-pouch Doc kept some of the necessary equipment for the doctoring chores which came his way. He thought this might be a case of acute appendicitis, in which case he would have to operate under primitive conditions. Not quite as primitive as the time on the Old Trail when he removed one by the light of a lantern and the aid of a bowie knife.

"You get those two ladies in off the street, wash them up and clean the scratches, they'll be all right after a rest," he said, and walked off with the woman.

"All right." Waco turned his attention back to the crowd. He swung his leg up forward, over the saddle-horn and dropped to the ground without the necessity of holstering his guns. "The fun's over now. Let's see all of you good people headed back to your homes."

"What?" Mrs. Harcourt screamed. "We came here to run those painted hussies out of town and that Libby Hogan attacked poor Mrs. Ryan without——"

"Without me Mary giving her a paste in the gob to start it?" Ryan finished for her. "That fool husband of your'n went in there and lost some money gambling. That's why you're stirring the folks up, not to get the girls out of town. Get on home all of yez. Come on now Molly Hennessey, and you, Katie Rafferty, yez saw a better fight there than ye'd get by paying good money to see. Now tote me Mary home and be thankful it wasn't no wuss."

"A fine thing," Mrs. Harcourt howled back, "and you Town Constable. I'll see you don't hold that job too long."

"Hold ye gob, ye ould hen," a plump cheery looking woman snapped, as she bent and took hold of Mary Ryan's feet, lifting them, while another obviously Irish woman, lifted her head. "It was you who wants ould Paddy here rather than pay some regular lawman good money to run the town. Well, oi'm satisfied with him."

"Sure!" the other woman grunted, as she held Mary up ready to carry her home. "Oi noticed that when Libby Hogan asked us who was going to throw her out that you kept well behind the other folks."

The crowd wavered, many of them noticed the same thing now it was pointed out to them. Waco watched them, noting Harcourt was still looking truculent. The man was almost as big as Ryan and much heavier than Waco, but it was fat, not muscle, for he looked more like a storekeeper than a hardrock miner.

"You folks just clear this street," Waco ordered, "or I'll jail every last one of you for disturbing the peace and inciting to riot."

"Fine thing?" Mrs. Harcourt hissed, seeing her supporters wavering. "A lawman and he's siding with the saloon crowd. It shows you how crooked——"

"I'm getting quick sick of talking." Waco's anger rose at this accusation. "I'm counting five and starting at three and any man who isn't headed for home then is going to jail."

Harcourt scowled. He was used, as the only storekeeper in Canvastown, to more respect than this.

"You're saying a lot with those guns in your hands," he growled.

Before the words were out of Harcourt's mouth Waco had spun the guns on his trigger-fingers and they were back in leather. Harcourt stared, then swung a clumsy punch. It had weight behind it, but that was all. It was slow and telegraphed to a fighting man who'd learned the fistic art under the Texas master, Mark Counter.

Waco's right hand came up, pushing the fist aside with

some contempt, then his left drove like a sledgehammer full into Harcourt's stomach. The big man gasped in agony and doubled over, dropping to his knees.

"One!" Waco said softly.

The crowd broke up. They knew that the Texan was getting riled and that painful as it must have been for Harcourt, the storekeeper had got off lightly to what the next man would get.

Ryan and Waco watched the crowd dispersing, the big Irishman grinning as he saw his wife carried into their tent by her two friends. Then they glanced at the saloon crowd who were helping the blonde away.

"You the town law, then, friend?" Waco asked, glancing at the man's gunless sides.

"Sure. The Harcourts were part of the bunch who elected me. Folks wanted to get a regular lawman, but they reckoned I'd come cheaper. They wanted to stop every bit of fun in the town, but I wasn't going to have that. Like today, Harcourt lost some money gambling and went home crying about it. So damned if his wife didn't stir up the folks. I thought we'd have us a full scale war, but my wife steps in. Trouble is she's an O'Toole and Miz Libby's a Hogan, and if you come from the old country you'd know what that means. Anyways, they got to fighting and before you could say knife the folks clean forgot about wrecking the saloon and was all sat back to watch the fight. I reckon Miz Libby knew they would and that's why she threw out the challenge, her being such a fine lady."

Waco could see that the Pinkerton man was wrong. Paddy Ryan might appear slow, but he had a quick mind and could see and think things out for himself. Then he grinned as he thought of how the fine lady had looked when she came through the wall of the tent.

A man rode towards them, a tall, handsome man wearing a white shirt, grey trousers tucked into riding boots and with a Merwin Hulbert gun in a shoulder holster under his right arm. The picture on the wanted poster had not been good, but for all that, Waco recognized him as being the man the Pinkerton Agency wanted, the man who was within two weeks of the Statute of Limitations wiping the slate clean for him.

Halting his big dun horse he looked first at the rip in the side of the tent, then turned his gaze on Ryan and Waco.

"What happened?" he asked.

Ryan explained, and the man who was now called Ace Turing laughed. He did not appear too worried by either the fight or what caused it, and seemed to take the same line as had Ryan. That the two women took what to them appeared to be the best way to avert more serious trouble.

"Hope they're not hurt too bad," Turing remarked.

"Divil a bit," Ryan replied. "Maybe a couple of black eyes between 'em and a whole lot of bruises, but nothing more serious. This here's a Ranger."

Turing swung down from his horse, holding out his hand to Waco. The grip was strong and firm, a man's grip. The way Turing met Waco's eyes told the young Ranger that there was no suspicion of his mission here in Canvastown.

"Like to see you, Mr. Turing," he said.

"The name's Ace to friends," Turing answered. "Come into my office."

They entered the canvas-built saloon, pausing just inside to look it over and see how much damage the two women caused in their fight. Apart from a broken chair and a couple of tables which had been overturned, but were now standing again, there was nothing to show that a first-class battle raged here a short time before.

"How's Libby, Mae?" Turing asked one of the girls.

"Resting. She's sore all over, but she'll be all right."

Turing laughed, then pointed to a door in the canvas side of the building opposite the holed wall. Opening this he waved Waco to enter the office first and followed, closing the door behind him. He walked by Waco, who stood with his shoulder against the jamb of the door and turned at his desk, remarking he hadn't caught the young Ranger's name.

"Waco." Taking out the poster and the warrant as he said it, the young Texan stepped forward and put them on the desk. Then he stood up with his right hand near the butt of his gun.

Looking down at the poster Turing shook his head, then slowly looked away up into Waco's eyes.

"Well?"

"I have to take you in. The Pinkertons want you. They sent me up here and if I don't take you back they'll likely send some bounty hunter after you. With me you'll get to Tucson alive."

"Two more weeks and I'd have been clear." Turing's voice was hardly more than a whisper. "That's all I wanted. Do you know, Waco, I didn't even know there was anything wrong with that cheque until the teller started yelling for the law. Then I panicked. I've never done another crooked thing in my life."

"Sure, this is one of the times I'd rather not be wearing a law badge. We'll pull out tomorrow morning, if that'll give you enough time to settle your affairs up."

"Tomorrow'll be fine." Turing looked the young man over, liking what he saw. "If you were one of the Earps I'd offer you a bribe to miss me for two weeks. I rode about for the Army and could disappear for a couple of weeks or more. But I know bribery would be no use with you. Make yourself at home, I'll be ready to go with you tomorrow."

Waco turned and opened the door. He drew back
slightly as he studied a man coming into the saloon. The
man was tall, wide-shouldered and good-looking, his face
reckless and gay in expression. From head to foot he was a
range country dandy, his clothes the height of cowhand
fashion. The shirt was open at the neck and through the V a
mass of curly black hair could be seen. He swept off his
hat, caught a girl by the waist and kissed her, then shook
back his head. His hair was black, short and curly.

"Howdy Curly!" Waco said softly, coming from the
door behind his cocked right-hand gun.

Curly Bill Brocious released the girl. She staggered to
one side out of the line of fire. The handsome young man
stood still, his hands just clear of his matched ivory-butted
Colts. He was fast, very fast, but against a man like Waco
he knew better than to try anything.

"Howdy, Waco." The voice and face were still cheerful
and friendly. "You still with the Rangers?"

"Sure, that means I've got to take you in. The Army's a
mite riled about those horses you took from their dealers."

"Figgered they might be."

The saloon crowd was tense and watchful, for they
knew that Curly Bill Brocious was not the sort of man to
submit tamely to arrest. He was Johnny Ringo's partner
and co-leader of the Rustlers, who made their headquarters
in the town of Galeyville, near Tombstone.

"Lift your hands, slow like, Bill," Waco ordered.

"I'm having me some bad luck," Brocious replied, not
making a move to obey the order. "First Torredos and Hernandez team up and are out there. I saw them and cut
round this way to keep clear of them. Then my hoss went
lame. Now this."

"You lifting your hands?"

"Sorry boy."

Waco saw Doc Leroy enter the saloon and stand behind Curly Bill. Even at that distance Waco could see the strain on his partner's face. Strain or not, Doc took in the situation and acted with speed. His right hand made a flicker and the ivory-handled Colt was in it. Brocious stiffened as he heard the click of the hammer coming back and he knew he was boxed in.

"Freeze solid, Curly," Doc warned, then to Waco, "call it a truce, boy."

"What do you mean?" Waco asked, crossing the room to disarm Brocious.

There was a deadly seriousness about Doc now which brought Waco to a halt without disarming the outlaw.

"Nobody's leaving this town for a spell. That kid I just looked at has typhoid."

"Typhoid?" Waco and Brocious repeated the last word, keeping their voices down.

There was an uneasiness in both men now. They were brave enough in the face of danger, armed men meant nothing to them. But typhoid was something again.

"Call it peace for a spell, Bill!" Doc suggested urgently.

"I've got nothing to lose," Brocious replied and spread his hands palm out in the sign of peace.

Doc and Waco holstered their guns. They knew the rustler would never break his word. Brocious never even made a move. He looked at Doc and waited to hear what was wanted of him.

Before Doc could say anything there was a commotion in the street and the Harcourts came in heading a deputation of townsfolk again.

"What is it with that child, mister?" Mrs. Harcourt asked. "Is it typhoid?"

"Typhoid?" A gambler came to his feet, panic written

on his usually expressionless face. "I'm getting out of here."

The panic hit the others, saloon and town folk alike. The crowd which had come surging in, passing by Doc, started to make for the door, but froze as that slim and deadly young man moved. One minute he stood there with empty hands, then almost before the eye could follow the move his gun was out and making an arc of the crowd.

"Nobody's leaving for a piece, except my partner and one man."

"Why them?" Harcourt appeared to have most of his wife's qualities and his voice was cracked. "Why should they go?"

"I want medical aid from Fort Lawrence."

The gambler's nerve was beginning to crack. He yelled, "Rush him, there's only one man there and he won't shoot."

"Yes, rush him," Harcourt yelled. "He's only one——"

"Two!" Waco's matched guns were out and he covered the crowd.

"Three." Ace Turing came from his office, blocking the panic from there.

"I counts four," Brocious put in, his guns in his hands, watching a man who was eyeing the torn wall. "Saw typhoid once, back in New Mexico. Some damned fool got spooked and ran. Carried it through three counties."

More people were crowding into the saloon now, listening to what was said and showing signs of panic, yet knowing those four men would not hesitate to kill anyone who tried to run.

Ryan and his wife came in. She still looked shaky and her left eye was swollen and nearly shut, but her face was grim and determined. She limped forward and glared at the scared-looking crowd, then asked:

"What's going on here?"

"Typhoid," Waco replied.

"Friend, you and Curly take four men you can trust not to run or spook," Doc put in before Waco could say another word. "Then I want every horse, mule and burro in camp corralled under my guard. I want either Curly Bill or you riding herd with two of the men on the corral day and night."

Ryan pointed out three men and Brocious called to a dark quiet man who was in the crowd. The six men headed for the door when a scared-looking man yelled:

"Nobody's going to take my hoss!"

Brocious turned, a mocking smile on his face. "We'll put that on your tombstone. Happen you try and take the hoss back."

Libby stood at the door of her quarters. She was wearing a housecoat over her underclothes and her right eye was blackened, but otherwise she looked all right. Moving forward, she flashed a look at Mary Ryan, a look more of friendly greeting than anything.

"What can we do to help, friend?" she asked Doc.

"Those folks want to be living in something better than a tent. That place across the street'd be fine."

"It's yours, though it needs cleaning up first," Libby answered, then turned to the girls. "Come on, all of you, there's work to be done."

"And who'll do it, might I ask!" Mary Ryan put in, a bunch of poorly-dressed women gathering around her. "Sure, you floozies never did any scrubbing except when you were in jail."

"We can try," Libby answered. "A pack of frowsy old hens like you can't go in there. It's a saloon."

"An O'Toole can go anywhere a Hogan can," Mary spat back. "And work twice as good as any painted huzzy.

Come on girls, let's show these dance hall biddies what hard work means."

The dance hall women and the Ryan bunch headed for the door, eyes glinting with anger and determination to show the other side how to work. Then the other women, all better dressed than the Ryan bunch followed. Only Mrs. Harcourt remained and Libby gave her a look of disgust, then ignored her.

"Good for Mary," she said smiling at Doc. "We'll get that place cleaned out for you, Joe," this to her swamper, "Get some water heating, hurry it."

Doc watched the women go and turned to see that their attitude was shaming some of the men for their previous panic. He had no time to waste though and gave his orders.

"I want a man who knows his way to Fort Lawrence. Waco's never worked this way before and I don't want any delays in him getting there. That means I want a man who can ride."

"Ace there rode dispatch for the army," the bardog called. "And he's the best man afork a hoss in this town, bar none."

There was some rumble of agreement amongst the men at this, although Harcourt and certain others did not appear to be any too happy with the arrangement.

"I've got a couple of Apache relay teams, Doc," Turing remarked. "That paint of Waco's looks to have been worked hard."

"All right, go and get them saddled ready," Doc answered. "You and Waco'll go."

"Why them?" Harcourt howled, panic in his tones. "Why should they go and we have to stay here?"

"We're getting out of here!" Mrs. Harcourt almost screamed out the words.

"No, you're not, ma'am. Old Curly Bill would shoot

down any man who tried to get a hoss from the corral," Waco warned.

"Curly Bill Brocious guarding the horses," Mrs. Harcourt snarled. "He'll take the best of them and light out the first chance he has."

"No he won't, ma'am," Waco put in softly. "I trust ole Curly. But you or every other man and woman in this town'd best listen to me now. If you run I'll hunt you down, me and every friend I have. No matter where you go we'll find you and when we do, be it man or woman, we'll hang them."

"The reason I'm sending two men is that way they've a better chance of getting through," Doc explained. "They'll be riding a relay team and that takes a hossman. I don't just mean a man who can sit on a hoss and let it do all the work."

"What danger is there out there that isn't in town?" Mrs. Harcourt moaned. She was scared of the typhoid, more scared than she'd ever been in her life before.

"Curly Bill told us Hernandez and Torredos have joined together and are working this ways," Doc answered. "Now I want all you men out there working hard. First, I want so many men, under our friend from behind the bar, to start filling in every backhouse hole and digging fresh pits. I want you, mister," indicating a tall, hard-faced man, "to take ten men and get that stream at the back of town unblocked. Dump all the rubbish you get out of the stream in one of the backhouse holes, pour kerosene over it, burn it and then fill in the hole. Then I want one man who can handle a paintbrush to make some signs to go round town. Who can handle it?" A man stepped forward. "Make it read 'Typhoid. Keep out', good and big. All right, gents, get to it."

By the time Waco turned his paint and Doc's black loose

and stored their gear in the Ryan tent, the men were working and from the saloon came the sound of scrubbing as the women removed the mud and dirt from the wooden floor of Turing's saloon.

Studying the two Apache relay strings, Waco liked what he saw. They were small, wiry animals, yet powerful and with all the heart in the world. It was this kind of horse which ran the grainfed cavalry horses ragged in the Indian campaigns, covering ground at a speed and for times which no cavalry horse could attempt to equal. The relay, three horses each, were trained to stick together. A man rode one and the other two would keep alongside it. Riding them alternately a man could cover ground far faster and for far longer than with just one horse.

The two teams were saddled and Turing was checking the saddles over. Waco joined him and found they were lightweight saddles and would not be as comfortable as his own Texas kak. However, when they got moving he would not have the time to change saddles every time he wanted to get afork a different horse. There was no saddleboot on any of the saddles, so Waco could not take his rifle along. Every ounce of weight could count and the rifle would be of no use to him this time. He retained his gunbelt and guns, for he knew the weapons might be of use to him.

Riding to the saloon door Waco and Turing waited for Doc to come out. He handed them two packages of food and a letter.

"Give this to the post surgeon, boy," he said. "Good luck."

Waco gripped his partner's hand so hard that Doc winced. "Same to you, amigo. We'll get there as quick as we can."

"I don't need telling that," Doc answered, but he spoke

to the rapidly departing backs of the two men and turned to go back into the saloon.

Inside, the women were all on their hands and knees, scrubbing hard. Libby Hogan and Mary Ryan worked side by side, sweat pouring down their faces and their aching, bruised bodies protesting as they forced themselves to work harder than all the other women.

"You two go see that all the drinking water is boiled before anybody takes any of it," he suggested.

"Let O'Toole here go, she needs an easy job," Libby gritted through her teeth.

"Both of you," Doc snapped before Mary could bring about the answer which rose.

They got to their feet and limped from the room side by side. Doc followed them and made a round of the town to see that all he'd ordered was being done.

Turing and Waco rode across the range country, travelling at a good speed and holding their horses to a pace which would best conserve their energies. There was a wagon trail to the Fort, but it wound around and was far from being the best going for a horse. Changing their mounts at frequent intervals they rode on and at nightfall Turing estimated they'd covered over a third of the journey. Waco twisted in the saddle, trying to get more comfortable, then he looked at Turing. "Can you find your way in the dark?"

"Sure."

"It'll likely kill your hosses if we keep going," the Texan warned.

"Rather the horses than the folk back in town."

"All right, we'll keep going then."

They rode on side-by-side, the Ranger and the man he'd come to take back to justice, or what the Pinkertons called justice. Neither spoke as he rode, for they concentrated on getting the most out of the horses. Dawn found them by a small stream and they allowed their mounts to rest for a time. Waco watched Turing, seeing the long, gruelling ride was having its effect on him. Turing had never ridden so far in many months, yet he did not complain. Waco was more used to spending hours at a time in the saddle. Once, on a trail drive, there was never a let-up for three days and nights, Waco having been in the saddle all that time, except when changing horses at the remuda.

They were just swinging into the saddles ready to cross the stream when Waco heard a noise behind him and turned, then without showing any emotion at all, said, "Don't turn, don't draw. We're being watched."

Five Mexicans rode from the scrub along the bank of the stream, four of them held Winchesters, the fifth, a squat ugly man, was unarmed, although he was belting a brace of ornate butted Colt 1860 Army revolvers. He halted his horse as the two men turned, a mocking sneer on his face.

"That's Torredos," Waco spoke from the corner of his mouth to Turing.

"Do we run, or fight?" Turing answered, eyeing the ornate dress of the squat man.

"Too late for either. Back my play," Waco replied. He raised a hand in greeting to the Mexicans. "Howdy, Torredos," he said cheerfully, "it ain't often we see you this far north."

Torredos studied these two trail-dirty men, noting their tired-looking horses and the hard look of them. Here would be no easy picking for his men.

"You know me?" he asked, pleased that his fame reached so far north.

"Saw you one time in Pasear Hennessey's place."

Turing did not know who Pasear Hennessey was, although he could see a slight change come over Torredos' face at the mention of it. Torredos knew that few gringos had heard of Pasear Hennessey's outlaw hideout which lay on a small island in the Rio Grande and was owned by neither the United States nor Mexico. Fewer still were the honest gringos who knew of it. Waco had learned of it from his friend, the Ysabel Kid, who, though an honest man now, had once been most prominent in the border smuggling business.

"So you know of Pasear Hennessey's place?"

"Sure, we're headed there now for a tequila and river-water."

Torredos smiled. His guess was correct. These two gringos were on the run from something. He looked pointedly at the horses and asked:

"You have ridden far?"

"Not far enough by a sight." Waco could see that his reference to the favourite drink at Pasear Hennessey's had convinced Torredos. "There's a troop of cavalry and a couple of Apache trailers back there. They're looking for us to be guests of honour at a cottonwood hoedown."

"That's why we're in a hurry," Turing went on. "Never did want to be found hanging around under a tree."

"Hanging around!" Torredos chuckled. "That is a good one, you must come and tell it to Joaquim. But why are they showing such an interest in you?"

"Funny thing that, they think that when we left the Fort sutler's place an Army hoss buyer's moneybelt followed us out," Turing answered and slapped his middle suggestively.

"Of course it did not and the dealer can prove it."

"Waal no, not in so many words." Waco liked the way Turing caught on. "See, somebody put a window in his skull."

"Not you, of course?" Torredos studied the bulge made by a well-filled moneybelt under Turing's shirt. "But if you did have the money what would you do with it?"

"Play poker." Waco could see the slight chance for them, for he knew that he could not ford the river in escape without getting shot and their only hope lay in this desperate chance he was taking.

"Poker." There was new interest in Torredos' eyes now. He could see a chance of getting rid of these two gringos with the aid of his partner Hernandez without having to share the loot. "So you play poker?"

"Been known to." Turing did not know what Waco was getting at, but he was willing to go along with it just the same.

"Then please accept my offer of a game. Not here." Torredos glanced back to try and see some of the non-existent posse. "At our camp."

"Why surely so," Waco agreed. "Just as long as it is across the river."

They were kept under the guns of the Mexicans as they crossed the river and the men never relaxed to give them a chance. However, they were not going out of their way as they rode along with Torredos.

The Mexicans were camped in a valley, or rather a drywash, for there was only the one opening. A Mexican bandit sat on a rock, rifle across his knees watching the range country. Just below the sentry, at the foot of the valley, was a picket-line with some thirty or so horses standing at it. A pair of big grulla stallions caught Waco's eye, they stood saddled, girthed tight and ready for riding. He nodded to them and Turing gave a slight inclination of his head to show what was meant.

"Leave your horses here, my men will attend to them," Torredos said.

Waco and Turing did not argue, they left the horses and walked towards a small cabin further down the wash. There a tall, elegantly dressed Mexican rose and looked them over.

"Friends of yours, Jose?" he asked cautiously.

"Good friends, Joaquim. They wish to play poker."

There was a covetous glint in Hernandez's black eyes as he called for a table to be brought and set up. He did not trust Torredos, in fact, there was little trust between either of them. His first thought was these gringos were brought in to get rid of him. Caution dictated that he called his men to watch the game. Torredos, no less trusting, gathered in his men. Waco saw this and knew there was a better chance of his getting away with it if Turing read the signs right.

The table and four chairs were set up. Waco and Turing sat facing each other, the Mexicans on opposite sides of the table, eyeing each other warningly. It was Hernandez who spoke when a greasy-looking deck of cards were put on the table in front of him.

"I think our guests would be happier with new cards," he said, not knowing how right he was.

There was a rumble of anger from the Torredos men, for the matter of cards was a touchy one with them. However, Torredos shrugged and called for a new pack, which was brought to him. He tossed it in front of Waco, who picked it up and broke the seal. The cards were all right, he guessed, as he ran his fingers along the edges and then riffled them through his hands. He passed them to Turing, who took them and with a gambler's feather-fingered care examined them, giving an almost imperceptible nod, which told Waco he also made the deck fair.

Yet Ace Turing still did not see Waco's plan here, nor understand how this would help them get away. He saw Waco lay a hand casually and apparently by accident flat on the table. Something in the way the young Texan looked at Turing made him reach up and lay a flat hand on his chest, too, the answer to the crooked gambler's signal for a partner. It was still a mystery to Turing, he knew Mexicans and could tell Waco also knew them. Why then was the young man going through with this. Even if they won all the money the two bandits possessed they would never be allowed to leave the camp with it.

Idly Waco shuffled the cards, knowing the attention of the two gangs of Mexicans were equally divided amongst watching their bosses and each other. Turing was studying the cards in Waco's hands, watching how he collected and retained four threes at the bottom of the deck. Then Waco put the cards on the table and casually Turing reached over to make the cut. He took the top half of the cards and placed them on the side nearest to Waco, who reached out, picked them up and replaced them as they were originally.

Then Waco started to deal, holding the cards in the crooked dealer grip, his index finger squaring the edges of the cards. Then while the other three fingers gripped the long edge the index was still holding the fore edge. The cards flowed out until it came the turn of Hernandez, then Turing saw the top card advance, one of the four threes slide from the bottom and the top card go back again. It was very well done, that bottom deal, and Turing, no cheat himself, admitted he'd rarely seen it done better.

The betting was steady, neither Waco nor Turing going it heavily, but Torredos pushed the pot to the limit. His face showed anger as his hand went under to the merciless threes. It was obvious Torredos for one could not mildly submit to losing.

It was then Turing knew what Waco was up to. He was an honest gambler, yet to protect himself from cheats he had learned how to handle cards in every crooked way.

Hernandez dealt the next hand, hitting another good one. Torredos looked even more annoyed and his men muttered to themselves. Waco sat back, knowing that if Ace Turing was thinking in the right way all would be well. He was. Waco promised himself not to play poker with a gent who could read signs as well as Ace Turing.

Torredos picked up a good hand, glancing suspiciously at Hernandez, who sat with an expressionless face, declining cards on the principle that he could hardly hope to better the 4, 5, 6, 7, 8, of hearts dealt pat to him.

The game went on, Hernandez being the heavy winner, his luck being well in as well as aided by the card manipulations of the Texans. Torredos, on the other hand, could not do a thing right. As often happens when a man hits a real bad run, Torredos was very unlucky. He could not seem to call anything right. If he played and the other men went along his hand failed, if he bluffed he was called. The only time he had a winning hand the others did not bet.

Turing now noticed a subtle change coming over the game and the spectators. There was tension in the air. Torredos grew more surly with every hand, Hernandez grew more cheerful, making bad jokes about his friend's poor playing ability. His men greeted each joke with gusts of laughter, but the Torredos followers scowled and fingered their weapons. The atmosphere around the table was electric now, one small spark would create an explosion.

Then as he reached for the cards Turing made his own sign, the sign a crooked gambler would make to warn his partner the time was on hand to take on suckers. Hernandez laughed as he counted his winnings from the last pot, several hundred of Torredos' dollars. Then Turing scowled and said:

"Hold hard, look here!"

Reaching out an apparently empty hand, Turing put it

under Hernandez' high-crowned sombrero which lay on the table. When the hand came out it held three cards.

With a snarl of baffled rage Hernandez threw back his chair, but with a cry like a tortured cougar Torredos hurled right over the table, his knife ripping up right into the other man's chest.

"Light out, Ace!" Waco roared as the two gangs started to fight.

Torredos came to his feet, a wild light in his eyes. He saw Turing grab up a big handful of the money from the table and turn to run for it. That was the last thing he ever saw. Waco's twin guns were out. Even in this moment he was lawman enough to make an end to a savage and vicious career by throwing a bullet into Torredos. Then Waco turned and sprinted after Turing, who was running at a respectable speed, even though he was stuffing money into his pockets.

The two fighting gangs ignored the two running gringos as they fought with each other, knives flashing and guns barking. However, the sentry at the head of the wash came bounding down the slope, his rifle came up and started to crash, sending dirt eruptions under their feet. Then he stopped and took more careful aim. At the same moment Turing and Waco also stopped, then both leapt. They went in opposite directions and the man hesitated, then threw a shot which caught Turing in the shoulder. Even as the gambler spun round he heard the thunder of Waco's matched guns. The Mexican seemed to be picked up and thrown backwards as the lead drew him on. Before the sentry's body hit the ground Waco had holstered his guns and was by Turing's side.

"Come on, Ace," he gritted. "Get afork one of those grulla hosses."

Turing staggered for the horse lines. The horses were

restive, but he managed to get the soup-plate horn of one of the grullas in his good hand. Sheer instinct got his foot into the big stirrup and he tried to haul himself into the saddle. Waco, knife in hand, was slashing the reins of the other horses as fast as he could, but he leapt forward and shoved Turing into the saddle, snapping, "Get out of here!"

The grulla sprang forward at a touch of Turing's heels and the gambler clung on as waves of pain went through him. Waco grabbed the other grulla and bounded into the saddle, then with a wild yell sent the other horses racing off. The other horses, at the yell and made restive by the fighting, broke and ran.

It was then that the two fighting groups broke off their battle and realized they'd been tricked. They fired shots after the two fast riding men, but their marksmanship was not great and neither Waco nor Turing were hit as they rode out of the wash.

After half a mile of fast riding Waco halted and turned to Turing who was hanging on to the saddle, trying to keep astride.

"I'll rough fix that for you," the young Texan said, "and rope you on the horse, too."

"If I can't stay with you, leave me," Turing answered weakly.

Doc Leroy walked along the line of beds in his temporary hospital, looking at the people who lay there. He was unshaven and looked as if he'd been missing sleep over the past six days since Waco left. In that time Doc had hardly seen his bed for more than a couple of hours at a time and he'd never taken his clothes off.

At the end of the room he turned and went to the door, opening it to hear what was getting to be a normal occurrence now:

"You fat old hag, just wait and I'll scratch your eyes out!"

"You and whose army?" Mary Ryan hissed back, shoving the hair from her eyes as she and Libby O'Toole stood scrubbing a pile of bedding.

They were like a couple of alley cats, quarrelling all the time, but Doc knew and they knew, it was only to help keep themselves on their feet. Of all the women in town none had worked so hard as Libby and Mary. They got only slightly more sleep than Doc himself and these arguments, threats and promises of what they would do to each other when they found time, were a means to fight off the tiredness which ran through them.

"Tired, Doc?" Libby asked with some concern as the young man came out.

"Seen times I felt better. How about you two?"

"Sure, we'll manage, won't we, Ryan?" Libby's brogue was suddenly as broad as Mary's own.

"That we will," Mary Ryan answered.

"I reckon we've held it," Doc remarked. "We haven't seen a new case in three days."

"You've done wonders, Doc," Libby said, straightening painfully. "When I think of what might have happened if you hadn't come——"

The words were stopped by angry voices in the street at the front of the building. Doc and the two women went through the hospital and out on to the street to find trouble starting.

Paddy Ryan stood holding the reins of the Harcourt buggy with one hand, while Harcourt lined his shotgun on the big Irishman. The storekeeper's face was a mask of wild panic as he yelled.

"Let loose of that rein."

Doc reached inside the door and took the Colt from his

gunbelt hanging on a hook just inside. He thrust the revolver into his waistband and snapped:

"Drop it or turn it this way."

Harcourt half turned, seeing the Texan standing there flanked by Libby and Mary. He saw that Doc Leroy wasn't holding a gun and snarled:

"We're getting out of here right now. We've not seen any help from the Fort and we're not stopping to die."

"Put it down, the Army should be here tonight or tomorrow," Doc replied.

"If those two went to the Fort——"

Doc's gun was in his hand, the hammer eared back and his arm thrown out to line the .45 muzzle right straight on the man. Harcourt was looking at death and he knew it. Doc was tired and he had been under a great strain for almost a week. It was only by exerting all his will power he didn't let the hammer of the Colt fall.

For an instant Harcourt hesitated, then Paddy Ryan acted, his face pale under the tan, yet knowing he must act or see Harcourt die. One big hand took hold of the shotgun, pulling it from the storekeeper's grip. The other hand bunched into a fist drove up with all Ryan's strength behind it, smashing full in Harcourt's fat, pallid face. Mrs. Harcourt screamed as her husband went over backwards into the rear of the buggy and Mary Ryan, her face showing the contempt she felt for the Harcourt family in general, snapped:

"Shut your mouth!"

"You stupid, half-witted fool!" Mrs. Harcourt shrank back before the venom in Libby's voice. "Don't you see that Paddy saved your husband. Doc's been driven hard for nearly a week and he nearly killed your fool man."

"Which same I'm going to do right now!"

Curly Bill Brocious came round the corner, his right-hand gun coming out in a flicker of movement. Harcourt stared frightenedly at the dark young rustler and let out a bleat of fear.

"Stop him, Ryan," he howled. "You're the law here."

"The lousy rat, he slugged young Nick back there at the remuda and took his hoss," Brocious growled. "There's one thing I can't stand and that's a hoss thief."

He was quite sincere. His acquiring the herd of horses destined for the cavalry did not come, in his mind, under the heading of horse stealing.

The crazy madness went out of Doc Leroy now and he shoved the gun back into his waistband.

"Easy, Curly," he said. "We stopped them."

"Easy hell, Doc," Brocious answered grimly. "We've been guarding the remuda all this time and near on every other man in town and woman has been working hard. Not this pair, they've been hid out in their tent. Then they go down to the corral and club that young Nick and leave him laying there. Paddy, give him that shotgun."

"Sorry, Curly," Ryan replied, watching the other man. "You could kill him even if he did have the shotgun. Leave him to us. Comes the end of this typhoid we'll run him out of town."

Slowly the anger left Curly Bill's face and his usual grin returned. He slid the gun back into leather, then moved closer. Harcourt cowered back yelling for Brocious not to hit him and Curly Bill laughed.

"You hit him, Paddy?" he asked.

"Sure."

"Nick'll be real pleased."

After Brocious walked back towards the remuda, herding the Harcourts and their buggy before him, Doc turned and smiled at Libby. He was relieved, for he did not expect Curly Bill to give in so easily.

A girl came from the canvas saloon. In her hand she held something Doc recognized, something he'd forgotten all about. Ignoring Doc the girl went straight to Libby, handed her the warrant and poster, then stepped back her face showing the anger she felt. Libby opened both papers out, looked down. Then her face paled and she staggered slightly. Instantly Mary Ryan put an arm around her, asking tenderly:

"What is it, Libby?"

"I found them in the office when I went in just now," the dance hall girl explained as Libby handed over the two documents.

Mary Ryan squinted down at the picture on the reward poster, then turned her eyes to Libby. For a moment neither spoke, then Libby raised a tortured face to Doc Leroy.

"So that's why you came here?" she asked.

"Sure."

"Are you still going to take Ace in, after all he's done?"

"That's what we were sent to do," Doc answered, not knowing himself what they would do when the time came. "Likely we'll——"

"Soldiers coming!" A man came running along the street, waving his hand and yelling at the top of his voice. "The soldiers are coming."

The warrant was forgotten now, everyone who could walk came running out and headed along the street, making for the edge of town. Alone of that wildly jubilant crowd Libby felt no pleasure, for ahead of the distant wagon a lone man rode towards them. She could recognize him. It was Waco. There was no sign of Ace Turing.

Then Libby felt a hand grip her arm firmly and looked. It was a hand which a few days before had gripped her hair just as firmly, tearing at it in that wild fight. Mary Ryan, still gripping Libby's arm, turned a flushed and angry face to Doc Leroy and asked bitterly:

"Where is he?"

Doc could only shake his head, he knew that whatever Waco decided, the young man would have brought Turing back to Canvastown first.

Waco came riding up afork an army horse. Behind him the patrol was halting outside town, only the medic's wagon would be coming in. Not knowing that the poster and warrant had been discovered, he rode up. Swinging down from the saddle he gripped Doc's hand, searching his friend's face for any sign of the disease and finding none.

"You all right, Doc?" he asked, with more feeling than Doc could ever remember hearing him use before.

"Sure, boy," Doc replied. "You look as if you could use some rest."

"Where's Ace?" Mary Ryan pushed forward belligerently. "You never left him in jail did you?"

"Now why would I do a fool thing like that, ma'am?" Waco answered with a disarming grin. "Old Ace kept acting like he thought I would, or should. Reckon it was getting that bullet in his shoulder when we hit Torredos and Hernandez that sent him loco. Anyways, I wanted him to stay in the post hospital, but he insisted on coming back on the medic's wagon. He tole me to give Miz Libby his love until he gets here in a couple of hours."

Saying this, Waco helped himself to the cigarette Doc had just finished rolling and was about to place in his mouth. Then taking the wanted poster and the warrant he extracted a match from his pocket, struck it on his pants and lit the paper. Waiting to get a good blaze going Waco lit his smoke and applied flame to the cigarette Doc rolled to replace the first.

Watching the paper burn, Libby said, "That was a Pinkerton poster."

"Shucks, ma'am, they've got plenty more," Waco answered. "Anyways, it won't do them no good at all."

"What do you mean?'

"Nobody is either leaving or coming into town for at least a couple of weeks, ma'am," Waco explained, "and by the time they can the Statute of Limitations will be effective. Ace will be clear. Then not even the Pinkertons can bother him."

"Just let them try it," Mary Ryan hissed, clenching her fists. "Just let 'em and me'n Hogan here'll scratch their eyes out."

"Reckon you'd do it too, ma'am," Waco remarked.

Two hours later the wagon came into town and Libby was reunited with Ace Turing. Not for long though. They were just kissing each other when Doc Leroy and the Army surgeon came up with orders for Turing to get into bed.

"Bed," Waco said, having been a smiling witness of the reunion. "Now that's a real pleasant word for a man to hear."

"And a woman," Libby sighed, watching Ace being taken to a tent where a bed was waiting for him. She looked at Mary Ryan, who was swaying with exhaustion by her side. "O Toole, I've got a big feather bed waiting in the saloon. I'd risk getting fleas off you if you dast come into the saloon and sleep in it."

"Fleas it is, Hogan?" Mary answered. "Sure, if you didn't look half dead right now I'd take ye by the hair and teach you what a real Irish fighting woman can do."

"When we've had some sleep I might even take you up on it," Libby answered, with a smile, then hooking her arm through Mary's, she headed for the bed.

Waco watched the women go into the saloon and thought that their feud was not nearly so serious as it first appeared when he and Doc arrived in town. He turned and found Ryan waiting to show him to a tent next to the saloon, where Doc was already laying fully dressed on a bed.

The celebrations of the town were postponed on orders from Curly Bill Brocious, Ryan and a couple of tough gents. Not that any of the quartet were averse to celebrating. Yet they held off for twenty-four hours while two women and two men slept in undisturbed peace.

Three weeks went by. The work begun by Doc Leroy and so ably carried on by the Army doctor, was showing its results now. The epidemic was broken and although there were new graves in the small cemetery the number was far less than it would have been without Doc's original handling.

Curly Bill Brocious, Waco and Leroy were standing in front of the saloon, just ready to leave, when the leader of the cavalry escort came up with five men. Before any of the three young men could do so much as wink, Curly Bill was covered by five Springfield carbines.

"All right, Brocious," the officer snapped. "Raise——"

"Brocious?" Waco looked puzzled, first at the officer, then at Curly Bill. "William, you surely wants to grow a beard. I'm sick and tired of folks taking you for Curly Bill Brocious."

"What?" the young lieutenant snapped, turning his attention to Waco. "You mean this isn't Curly Bill?"

"I'm a Ranger, mister," Waco answered. "Would I be stood here like this, talking to a wanted man."

"But I was told——"

"Some damn fool's been jobbing you," Waco growled.

"Wish folks wouldn't show their sense of humour. Going and fooling a soldier of our glorious cavalry thataways. Can you see a mean cuss like that ugly ole Curly Bill staying on here and helping folks out?"

"No," the officer agreed. "I can't. Who are you, sir?"

"This here's Mr. Graham," Waco introduced, before the grinning Brocious could reply. "Lives over Cochise County way. Served as Deputy Tax Assessor for the county one time."

Waco offered a fervent prayer that the young lieutenant did not know the full story of how Bill Breakenridge, the Cochise County deputy sheriff asked Bill Brocious to ride with him on a tax collection of the various ranches in the rustler infested hill country. Curly Bill went along, not only that, but insisted that even the rustler gangs paid up their taxes, too.

The officer was new from the East and did not know the story. His sergeant could have enlightened him. The sergeant's name was O'Toole and he had a sister in Canvastown. This same sister saw to it that Sergeant O'Toole kept his mouth tight shut.

"Well, if you're ready Mr. Graham," Doc said. "We'll head off out."

Three horses stopped on the rim and three riders looked back at Canvastown. Curly Bill Brocious held out his hand, shaking with the two Rangers.

"If you ever need a friend or I can do anything for you either come to Galeyville or send word there," Brocious said. "Adios, see you down the trail."

"Adios, Bill, don't let the Earps get behind you," Waco answered.

Doc Leroy watched Brocious ride away, then turned to his partner.

"I might be wrong," he said, rubbing a hand over his jaw. "But ain't helping a wanted man escape agin the law?"

"Don't know. Reckon it might be though."

"Then happen we'll have the Pinkertons after us," Doc drawled and started his horse towards Tucson.

CASE SIX

Some Knowledge of the Handgun

"You always were real lucky, boy," Doc Leroy eyed his partner, Waco, sardonically. "Look at the way you got Torredos and Hernandez and bust up their bunch."

Waco eased himself in the low-horned, double-girthed Texas kak saddle. He grinned like an amiable schoolboy as he replied, "We could use us some luck right now. Say like finding some sign of the Apache Kid. We've been out for well over a week without seeing hide nor hair of him."

Doc thought over his partner's words for a moment, allowing his big black horse to walk at an easy pace alongside Waco's seventeen-hand paint stallion.

"Don't reckon it'll worry Cap'n Bert if we don't find the Kid," he remarked. "We were only sent out to stop you stomping Strogoff. I thought you would when he asked you how much Curly Bill gave you to turn him loose and get him by the Army."

Waco tried to look penitent but failed badly. He looked more like a mischievous boy than ever. "I'd do it again for the same reasons, Doc. And I surely won't lose any sleep over what Pinkerton or any of his dirty bunch think about me."

Doc chuckled, remembering the stormy scenes at Ranger Headquarters when they returned from their last assignment. They returned to Tucson, not only without bringing in the man they'd been sent to arrest, but having also released Curly Bill Brocious after taking him. More than that they helped Brocious escape from an Army patrol which was about to arrest him for stealing a bunch of remounts destined for use of the cavalry.

Strogoff found out most of this and raged about it. Captain Mosehan, knowing the full story, agreed with his men that they'd acted in the only way possible under the circumstances. He also admitted that under similar circumstances he would have done just what they did. So Strogoff was forced to snarl and rage about Ace Turing avoiding the Pinkerton Agency and now being cleared under the Statute of Limitations.

It was more to avoid trouble than any other reason that Mosehan sent his two fire-eating young Rangers out in an attempt to track down and locate the Apache Kid. Mosehan knew that the way things were going Pinkerton would need a new head for his South-west Branch if Strogoff failed to stay clear of Waco, for matters were fast getting to the point where only gunplay could end them.

The hunt for the Apache Kid, like most others for that elusive red gentleman, was not successful. The Kid came and went like a ghost, crossing and recrossing the range like a wraith, travelling as only an Apache warrior could. For some time there had not even been a report of anything like an Apache Kid killing, so the search was taking on an aspect of a hunt through a haystack, looking for a needle. The two Rangers searched hard for a week without finding any trace and now were on their way to the town of Hannibal, where, unless orders awaited them from Mosehan, they would stay for a few days, resting the horses before going first to the town of Bellrope, then back to Tucson.

The horses walked slowly up a slope and halted at the top. Waco and Doc looked down to where a small ranch house nestled at the foot of the slope in front of them. It wasn't a large place, just a cap and ball outfit, but from the neat way it was cared for it would grow. The corrals and the couple of outbuildings showed care and attention in their construction. The ranch house, though small and containing, from all appearances, both cookshack and bunkhouse of the crew, was freshly painted.

It was the corral which attracted the attention of the two Rangers, or the three men who stood arguing outside it. Though too far away to hear what was being said it was obvious that the men were not in agreement about something.

Two of the men, the pair facing towards Waco and Doc, were cowhands from their dress. The other was a gambler or his grey, cutaway, tight-legged trousers and town shoes lied.

Suddenly the gambler's hand went to his side and one of the pair of cowhands brought out the gun from his holster, firing two fast shots. The gambler spun round, lurched and fell on to his face. The second hand dropped to his knees beside the body, then glanced up the slope, pointed and yelled something to his friend. The cowhand, who was still standing with the gun smoking in his hand turned and ran to where a cowhorse stood fastened to the corral rail. Tearing loose the reins the cowhand went into his saddle and headed out fast.

"Take them two, Doc!" Waco ordered. "I'll get him!"

Doc sent his black down the slope without any argument. If the shot man was only wounded he could do far more than Waco down there. Doc's attention was on his partner, not on the man who still knelt by the gambler down there by the corral.

Swinging his paint off at a tangent Waco sent it barrelling down the slope like the devil after a yearling. The huge stallion stretched out like a racehorse and covered the ground with the sure-footed stride of a Rocky Mountain sheep avoiding hunters. Waco rode with easy grace, helping the horse all he could and blessing the chance which made him select the paint from Clay Allison's remuda. He'd taken the horse in the first place because Dusty Fog, his hero, rode a paint. Since then Waco never found cause to regret the choice. Particularly was the paint suited for law work, for it was bred for the rough and tough western style of racing which meant going for miles at a good speed. The other man was riding a little dun cutting horse. The race was far from an even match. At herd work the dun would run rings round Waco's big paint, but in an open chase it was outclassed.

Looking back over his shoulder, the cowhand saw his pursuer rocketing after him, then without using his spurs tried to get more speed from the little cutting horse. Eagerly the little animal responded, giving all it had, willing to go on giving until it collapsed. However, it was no use, and with every long and raking stride the paint was closing up on the other horse.

Under Waco's left leg reposed a Winchester Continental Rifle with a calibre of 45.75, which could outrange the older model of '73 rifle the cowhand carried in his saddle-boot. There were many lawmen in the west who would have drawn the rifle and ended the chase with a single well-placed 350 grain bullet. Waco learned his law work under a man who would tolerate no such thing. A man whose rule was, never draw unless forced, then shoot to kill and keep shooting until the man was dead.

Allowing the paint to close in on the other horse, Waco watched for the first sign that the other man meant to fight. Until that cowhand made a move towards his gun Waco would not attempt to draw his own. He could see the little horse was tiring and knew the cowhand would stop soon.

It was only a couple more minutes after that the young cowhand's horse staggered. Instantly he slowed it down, swinging it round in a tight circle and dropping his hand towards the butt of his gun.

Waco's left hand dipped and the staghorn-handled Colt came out into it, lined with the hammer drawn back. "Ranger here!" he snapped. "Drop it."

"Ranger?" The young man lifted his hands shoulder high. "All right, Ranger, I quit. There's no sense in killing a good cutting hoss, that paint of your'n can run faster'n a Neuces steer."

Waco slowed the big paint and it knew what was expected of it, moving towards the other animal, watching it all the time. Waco brought the horse to a halt alongside the man and held out his hand.

"Hand over your gunbelt."

The cowhand was a tow-headed young man, good-looking and cheerful featured. His range clothes were good quality, showing that he was a man who cared for his appearance and bought the best. Waco guessed he was the owner of the spread, the most rare of creatures, a cowhand who'd saved enough to make it pay.

He unbuckled the gunbelt carefully with his left hand, then passed it across to Waco, who accepted it.

"Look, Ranger, I thought Mason had a gun when I drew on him."

Waco strapped the gunbelt to his saddlehorn with the gun away from the side nearest the cowhand. He'd seen at first glance the gun was not a Colt, and now he could see it was a Smith and Wesson. The gun was one of the new models the latest pattern double-action model, unless he missed his guess. He looked at the young man and replied:

"Head back to your spread. If he was armed you'd no need to run."

They rode back to the spread at an easy pace, neither speaking. Waco holstered his gun as soon as he disarmed his prisoner. Somehow he did not think he would have any trouble from the cowhand. The young man was no fool and would not try a barehand attack on an armed man who'd already shown how fast he could handle a gun. Even the saddlegun was no use to the cowhand, for long before he could reach down and draw it Waco could get his own gun out and into use.

The matter, so far as Waco was concerned, was at an end. He'd seen the shooting and to him it looked to be fair and above board. In that case there would be no serious charge to be made. On the other hand, if the gambler was not armed it would hardly be more difficult. Just a matter of arranging the trial, appearing as witness and then riding on again. All in all it was an open and shut case. Doc Leroy was standing by the body. He was alone and a second horse which had been tied by the cowhand's mount was also gone.

"He's as dead as I've ever seen," said Doc. "Hit twice, shoulder and back."

"Twice?" Waco remembered hearing the two fast shots.

"Sure, we heard two shots," Doc answered as his

partner swung down from his paint and walked towards the body.

Waco bent down, glancing at the hole in the man's jacket back. The blood had not yet soaked through on to the grey material. There were black powder marks round the edge of the hole. This was to be expected, for the two men were close together and a black powdered bullet threw a considerable amount of residue out.

The other wound was high in the shoulder, merely a graze and a tearing of the jacket. Waco looked at the edges of the tear, noticing how it widened at the back. Then he noticed something more and raised the body slightly to look at the underside of the tear. Then with his curiosity satisfied he straightened up and turned to Doc.

"Where at's the other hand?"

"Headed for town to tell the marshal," Doc replied. "I didn't see any reason to hold him here and he wasn't the sort I'd want to stand talking to."

"The gambling man armed?"

"Nope, though he's got a gunbelt and holster with him. No gun though." Doc had not disturbed the body any, except to check that there was nothing he could do to help.

Waco's eyebrows drew closer together. There was a puzzled glint in his eyes, for he smelled something bad in this entire business. He could see that he might be wrong and this would not prove to be the open and shut case he'd first imagined.

"All right, friend, tell it," he snapped.

The young man, still sitting his horse, looked badly shaken by Doc's news. He swung down, looking at the still form on the ground, then told his story.

"I'm Bill Tench, this's my spread here. I bought it a few months back with money I'd saved working for ole Texas John. The other feller was Joey Smith, he's my segundo and hand, ain't got but the one yet. This here was Ben Mason, he runs the game in Hannibal. A couple of weeks back he skinned Joey out of a month's pay, so I got a bunch of my pards and we went round there. I took Mason and his two gunmen on and whupped all three of them. That caused some bad blood between me and Mason and I told him to keep well clear of me out here. Then this morning he comes out and tells me Joey lost his share of the spread in the game last night."

"Had he?" Doc inquired.

"I own this place, just me. Joey came along with me when him and Texas John had a falling out. I took him on to work for me but he wasn't my partner. That's what I told Mason. He called me a liar and made like he was going for his gun. That was when I pulled on him."

"Why'd you run?" Waco asked.

"Damned if I know. Johnny yelled the law was coming and that Mason wasn't toting a gun. Then I saw you two coming and lit out."

"Why?"

"Man wasn't wearing a gun," Doc reminded his partner.

"Sure, that was what Joey told me. I saw the gunbelt and figured he must be, that was why I drew on him."

"Why run out, then?" Waco carried on doggedly.

"Friend, I've been punching cattle down Cochise County way, riding for ole John Slaughter. I know what sort of a break a cowhand can expect from lawmen like the Earps. With them I'd have been real lucky to get asked to halt before they gunned me down. Then when I saw you wasn't wearing a badge and that I'd kill that ole Sam Moss and still not tire your paint I quit. I reckon I must have spooked at first, never killed me a man before."

Doc watched his partner, for he knew Waco better than almost any other man and could see something was worrying the young Texan. Waco was going over everything he'd seen and heard, working on it like a dog worrying at a bone. Doc knew better than ask what was on Waco's mind and waited to hear what was said next.

"Doc, you and Bill here best load the body on to a hoss and we'll take it to town with us. Reckon the local law'd best handle this."

While Doc and Tench did as they were asked, Waco stayed where he was, not offering to go and help them. Instead he took the Smith and Wesson from the holster and turned it over in his hands, comparing it with the balance of his own matched Colt guns. Ignoring the two he broke the revolver, lifting out all the shells. Only two had been fired and he dropped all of them, fired and loaded, into his pocket. Then he closed the gun again, gripped the butt and hefted it. The balance was different from the Colt Peacemaker, nor did the handle point so naturally. He guessed that on a draw the gun would tend to send its charge high.

Frowning, Waco looked down at the gun, for he knew guns well. In his life he'd handled a great many firearms of all kinds, though mostly they were single action and needed cocking before they could be fired. With the new model Smith and Wesson a pull on the trigger took back the hammer automatically. This would make the Smith and Wesson slightly faster to fire than the Peacemaker. It was something Waco didn't like.

He snapped the trigger twice, fast, then repeated the movement. Doc and Tench were finished loading the body now and they stood watching him. Both knew that it was more than idle curiosity which compelled Waco to handle the gun in this manner. He went to the corral, trying to read from the signs on the ground more of what was worrying him, but there was no chance of doing so, for the soil was far too hard here.

"When you all finished playing sheriffs and robbers we're waiting," Doc said sarcastically as he watched Waco clicking the gun again.

"Sure." Waco went to his paint and swung into the saddle, then shoved the Smith and Wesson back into the holster. He offered no explanation for his actions, but just jerked his head and said, "Let's go."

Hannibal City was getting set for a night of revelry, the sun sinking down behind the hills warning the business men that soon the hands would be coming in from the spreads and Hannibal would boom again. In fact, some of the hands were already in town, at the bar of the First, Last and Only Chance saloon.

The name city was rather grandiloquent, for the twenty or so houses which made up the metropolis of Hannibal. The street was not overcrowded, for the houses were spaced well apart, not on any snobbish motive but because there was plenty of room to build. The three shops, the marshal's office and jail were the sole reason for the town being here, the local ranches supplying most of the custom which came their way.

A small bunch of loungers outside the saloon rose as Waco and Doc rode in with Tench and leading the horse with a blanket covered shape thrown over the saddle. Even smaller was the bunch who came off the porch and followed them towards the small building which housed the undertaker.

A small, fat, cheerful-looking man stepped from the building, which was also a store. He glanced at Tench, then at the still shape, and with no show of emotion said, "Bring him in here, please. You can lay him on the bench. I started to make a box when I heard Mason rode out there this morning. Figgered I'd need it one way or another."

"Take off his coat, friend," Waco put in. "I'm a Ranger and I want that coat for evidence."

The town marshal came in while the coat was being removed. He was a small, tough-looking old-timer with a long, flowing moustache and quick, bright eyes. From his clothes he was not rich and that meant he was probably honest. He nodded a greeting, watched Waco sling the coat over his arm, then asked, "You are two Rangers?"

"Why, sure," Waco agreed.

"Best come down the office then." The marshal's tones were reserved, neither friendly nor antagonistic. His eyes were more friendly when he turned to Bill Tench. "Come on, boy."

It was a small office, not even as large or comfortable as Captain Mosehan's spartan establishment in Tucson. It was only one room attached to the jail, which looked strong enough to hold in a very weak, one-armed midget.

"The name's Ted Hanks," the marshal said as soon as they entered and took the rickety chairs to sit at the desk. "Real pleased you brought Bill in alive."

Doc stamped hard on Waco's foot, stopping the young man's angry words, and growled, "We allus try to bring them in alive. Captain Mosehan likes it that way."

"No offence," Hanks grunted, noting the anger in the faces of the two Texans. "So you pair are Rangers. You look like you can handle it all right."

"We try." Waco accepted the apology.

Hanks turned his attention to Bill Tench and shook his head sadly. "So it come to this, did it, Bill?"

Tench shook his head worriedly. He still looked dazed and wondered what Waco wanted the coat for. It must be evidence against him and that meant these two soft talking, friendly-acting men did not believe him at all.

"I don't know what went wrong," he answered. "All I

know is Mason come out to my place and told me he'd won Joey's share. Then when I said Joey wasn't a partner he called me a liar and reached down. I drew on him because I thought he was armed."

"That figgers," Hanks agreed.

In the West a man never used the word liar, unless he was ready, willing and able to reach down for his gun real fast and back his words with hot lead. Waco could see that if this ever came to a trial a good lawyer would make much of this statement. Then he heard what Hanks said next.

"That's not the way Joey Smith's been telling it around town."

"How's Smith telling it?" Waco asked, all attention again.

"Allows Bill waited until Mason turned to walk away, then shot him in the back."

Tench lurched forward, his hands clenched so hard the knuckles showed white. "Why would he say that?" he asked. "Mason was facing me when he made his move. I don't know how the bullet got into his back."

"Not the way Smith's telling it, boy. He's told me and near on every other man in town you hit Mason in the back. Started trying to stir up some bad feeling, but none of the cowhands round here are going to do anything foolish. They know you and they like you. There's only Mason boys who might try and start something."

"But he's lying in his teeth," Tench yelled. "I tell——"

Hanks was looking down at the jacket, his attention on the hole in the middle of the back.

"I thought that all along, Bill. But that hole looks real bad and there's some it won't please to think you didn't shoot Mason down in cold blood. I warned you against that drunken no-good all along. Any man Texas John sets afoot and fires ain't wuth his keeping. Smith never took to you saving your money when he was off drinking and bucking the tiger, and he didn't take to you buying that spread. I knew there'd be trouble when you took him on. Even had to take his gun off him last night when he came in to town and started raising hell."

Before Hanks could go on further with what he was saying, the door of his office crashed back and two big, burly men swaggered in. They had all the appearance of a prime pair of range bullies and their low-tied guns showed much use.

"You got Tench?" the taller of the pair growled. "Good, now we'll take him off your hands and save the county the cost of a trial."

"That's right," the second went on, eyeing Hanks. "So you just turn him over to us nice and peaceable, Ted, and there won't be no trouble at all."

Hanks scowled and started to get to his feet, but before he could it was Waco who spoke up.

"He's our prisoner."

The two hard-cases studied the two Texans, who were now on their feet. Then the taller of them spat on the floor.

"We still wants him."

Waco and Doc moved forward so they stood between the two men and Tench. They stood there with that relaxed-looking stance which was a sign they were more than ready to handle things.

"Then reckon you'll just have to try and take him," Doc drawled gently.

"These boy badges are some lippy, Mr. Ackers," the taller man sneered.

"Lippy as muley cows, Mr. Pollan," Ackers agreed. "Do we show them how it's done by us?"

Saying these words Ackers made his move, dropping his hand hip-wise just slightly ahead of Pollan.

Waco and Doc's action was even faster and showed that they were completely unaware of the honour Ackers and Pollan were doing them in showing how it was done. The end product was that they stood unalarmed, unshown, unafraid and behind their cocked and lined Colt guns.

Ackers and Pollan stood very still.

For a moment the two Rangers stood with their guns out, letting their control of the situation sink into the hard and not usually receptive heads of Mr. Ackers and Mr. Pollan. Then the guns whirled back into leather with the same prestidigial skill they made their appearance.

"You are still wanting our prisoner?" Doc inquired mildly.

"If you do say the word and carry right on," Waco agreed. "If you don't you'll find the door right where you left it. Reckon it opens as easy from this side as the other."

Pollan studied Ackers and Ackers reviewed Pollan, reading indecision in each other's face. Neither were willing to make any hostile demonstration against the two Texans and see if they were as accurate as they were fast. They turned to go out of the door, but Pollan decided speech was called for and looked back over his shoulder to make the said speech.

"Folks round here won't like this. No matter what Hanks tells you they'll want to see this killer hang."

"Folks don't allus get what they deserve," Waco reminded him.

"Else I'd be President of the Confederate States of America and riding in a coach," Doc finished for his partner. "But I reckon that some place in this wicked world there's someone who wants to see you pair more than we do."

"Doc, being so polite and well brought up, don't like to say this." Waco's mocking tones were charged with menace. "But we're quick sick of the sight of both of you. Now if you've got a play, make her. If not, fade."

"All right, we're going," Ackers growled, opening the door. "But folks won't like it when they hear."

"We mourns for them before and after's," Waco answered. "Drift!"

The door closed far more gently than it opened for Mr. Ackers and Mr. Pollan. Hanks looked at the door for a moment, then at the two Rangers. There was a new respect in his eyes now and he wiped his face with a bandana, then remarked:

"I never saw Ackers and Pollan back down that easy afore."

"Them the gambler's two hired guns?" Doc asked, and when Hanks nodded, went on, "I never yet saw two guns so keen to back up a dead man. Thought they'd be headed out looking for a new boss now the pay stops."

Waco went to the window and watched the two men enter the saloon. "Anything to that lynch talk?" he asked.

"Nope, not for Bill here there ain't," Hanks replied. "Ackers and Pollan just thought they might be able to bluff me into handing over Bill."

"You scare 'bout as easy as Waco here," Doc drawled. "And you seen him just now. He's a bundle of nerves."

"What was you saying about Smith's gun?" Waco asked suddenly.

"Took it off him last night," Hanks replied and lifted a worn Colt Civilian Peacemaker from the drawer of his desk. "He was howling for war and all set to get hisself killed by Mason's guns."

Waco picked up the Smith and Wesson gun from the table and stuck it in his waistband. "Let's go get us a meal, Doc," he suggested.

"All right, boy." Doc was used to his partner by now. "I

feel a mite gut-shrunk myself. Say, where's that hombre Smith at?"

"Down to the saloon, been there all day holding the bar up," Hanks replied.

"*Bueno,*" Waco jerked a thumb towards the jacket on the table. "Take care of that, although I don't reckon we'll need it any."

"Sure, how about Bill here."

"Best let him stay a spell. See you."

The saloon was busy as Waco and Doc pushed open the batwing doors and went through, halting to look around. The cowhands at the tables and the bar were all noisy and seemed happy enough. There was none of the hard-drinking or the sullen, brooding silence that usually went with a lynch mob. One man alone at the bar did not appear to be part of the happy groups around. He was a sullenly handsome young cowhand, his clothes worn and dirty, his boots run over at the heels and his face unshaven. He stood there looking down moodily at the empty glass in his hand. The bardog caught the inquiring look this man gave and with a contemptuous gesture picked up the bottle, then hammered home the cork with the heel of his hand in a sign that the man's credit was nonexistent.

Waco saw this byplay, then observed Ackers and Pollan standing by the door of the backroom and watching them. Apparently the two gunmen had made good use of their time and were outside a couple of strong snorts of brave maker. They advanced across the room. Pollan was the nearest and he asked in a loud voice, "What the hell are you after here?"

"Neither you or your partner," Waco replied.

Pollan considered his reputation in the town, then he considered that guns were not the answer to the question.

He could see the cowhands were watching him, waiting to see what he intended to do. Considering this, he made his move. A hard swung punch. The result was no more satisfactory than his previous attempt.

There are two ways of performing the flying mare throw of wrestling. The gentle way is to lever the arm down so the joint is able to bend while the throw is being made. The other way was how Waco did it. His head moved aside and his hands came up to catch the wrist, twist it so the elbow joint was on his shoulder. Then he levered hard. Pollan appeared to be taking wings, he had to go or break his arm.

Lunging forward, Ackers was about to help his friend who just lit down with a bone-jarring thud. A slim, pallid-faced, studious shape was in front of Pollan and a soft, Texas voice asked, "You wanting something, friend?"

"Nope, nothing at all," Ackers replied, halting, his proposed course of operation holding no attraction for him now.

Waco and Doc strolled on to the bar, knowing all eyes were on them. A man rose and greeted them. He was an old acquaintance from their cowhand days and introduced them to his friends at the bar.

"That's Smith," Doc remarked softly, pointing to the sullen man who was now staring at his empty glass.

Waco glanced at the man, noting his generally untidy dress did not go with the ornate, silver-mounted, ivory-butted Peacemaker which rode rather high in his holster.

The talk turned to the shooting and although most of the cowhands at the bar didn't agree with Waco and Doc bringing Tench in, none of them appeared to think he was guilty of murder.

Waco took the gun from his waistband, showing it to the

cowhands and saying, "This's the gun Bill used. Any of you boys ever seen it afore?"

"Sure," a man replied. "I saw him with it a few days back, just after he bought it. Was real proud of it. One of them new-fangled double-shooting guns, ain't it?"

"Sure," Waco agreed.

"Don't like them much," another of the men put in.

"Or me," Waco agreed, seeing his chance and getting the opening he'd been hoping for when he brought the gun along with him. "They get off their shots too fast for me."

"Don't see that," the one who'd recognized the gun objected.

"Tell you though," Waco ignored the question for the minute. "Mason and Bill Tench weren't friends. Yet when Mason went out there to see Bill he wore a gunbelt but didn't have a gun in the holster."

Ackers and Pollan were at the bar now, at the far end. Pollan opened his mouth to say something, but Ackers shook his head. Smith was looking along at Waco with eyes that were fast becoming sober and scared.

"So Mason didn't have a gun?" he growled.

"I don't see how a man could get his shots off so fast," the young cowhand put in, eager to learn about guns from an acknowledged master like Waco.

"Mind, one time when I was riding for Clay Allison," Waco explained. "Ole Clay's real good with a gun as you'll likely all know. Well, this gunhand went after Clay and they drew. Clay's real fast, but he can't use two guns at the same time. Fact is, I ain't seen but Dusty Fog who can. Well, ole Clay drew and shot left, then right a damned sight faster than I just said it. The first shot hit the gunny in the shoulder up high. Just touched him and ripped through his coat, but it spun him right round and the other bullet caught the gunny in the middle of the back."

Smith's face was ashy pale. He stared at Waco and opened his mouth to say something, then lurched from the bar. He'd hardly taken more than a couple of steps when Waco spoke again.

"I thought the marshal took your gun from you, Smith," he said. "That's a real fine one you're wearing."

Smith came round, his hand going down to the gun-butt. Waco's matched guns were out before the move was made. The right hand threw a bullet which just grazed Smith's shoulder, spinning him, and on the tail of the bullet Waco's shot tore Smith's cheap woolsey hat off from behind.

"That's how it happened out at Bill Tench's place," Waco told the crowd. "I knew Bill hadn't shot Mason in the back as soon as I saw the hole in his coat. It carried powder burns but the wound at his shoulder didn't. Not at the back anyhow. It did at the front. Then I knew what'd happened. I almost guessed at the rest of it when I saw the empty holster. When I heard Smith lost his gun the night before, I knew I was right. He took the gun, pushed it into his holster while Doc was watching me. Thought I'd likely kill Bill, or that Ackers and Pollan would get their revenge on him for licking them."

"Thought it was strange, a man going to see an enemy wearing a gunbelt and no gun," Doc admitted. "That'd be asking for trouble."

"Sure," Waco agreed. "I thought Smith might have thrown the gun away and was going back to make a search for it after I brought it in. Then when I saw that gun in Smith's holster, I knew I needn't bother. It's one of the Artillery models, like mine, with a five and a-half inch barrel. Smith's holster is made for the Civilian model, with the four and three-quarter inch barrel. So the gun rode high in the holster."

"What you going to do with Smith, Ranger?" a man asked.

"Nothing we can do, much," Waco replied. "It's left to Bill Tench. Reckon that Smith's going to set afoot again."

Bill Wendee Likes an Edge

The town of Bellrope, Arizona Territory, was blessed with a long-haired, two-gun terror. Bill Wendee rode in one day, coming from the east, astride a fine-looking claybank with a fancy Cheyenne roll saddle inlaid with silver.

The possession of such a man as Wendee did not cause any great rejoicing in the quiet little county seat, even though he made a fine figure of a man as he strode around amongst the more quietly dressed fellows. Six foot tall he stood, although the shining, high-heeled boots with the great Spanish-style spurs made him look even taller, and the high-crowned, snow-white Stetson hat added more inches to his stature. He was wide of shoulder and his carriage was graceful, while his shoulder-long hair and sweeping moustache reminded the older men who knew him, of Wild Bill Hickok, the late, though not lamented Kansas lawman. He wore a fancy buckskin shirt and the long flowing, sky-blue bandana hung almost to the waist of it, where the wide Sioux wampum belt supported his skin-tight grey trousers. The trousers were so tight they could hardly have been comfortable and were tucked without a crease into the boots. Around his waist was a shining black gunbelt supporting matched pearl-handled, nickel-plated Colt Cavalry Peacemakers. From his back, in a cunningly devised sheath, was a bowie knife with a saw edge.

Who he was and where he came from no man in this town asked him. That was never done in the old West, for a man was free to come and go where he pleased. There were rumours about him, varying from the mocking that he was a rich dude who'd fallen in love with a girl in Buffalo Bill Cody's show and now come west to try and find her again, to the suspicious, which had Sheriff Daniel Hendricks going through his "wanted" posters trying to decide which men would look like this with the aid of long hair and a moustache.

For his part, Wendee stayed at the Hotel, paid his account regularly and apart from pistol whipping a cowboy who made fun of him, caused no trouble at all. He might have lived out the rest of his days there, accepted, if not respected, if love had not come his way.

At least, love might be the term for what he felt for Connie Hendricks, the pretty red-haired daughter of the sheriff. He'd seen her on her way to school, where she helped Martin Aimes, the teacher. Whatever his feelings might have been towards her, there was no doubt about how she felt where he was concerned. With the range-bred woman's distrust of such a fancy-looking dresser she never gave him any encouragement whatsoever, preferring Martin Aimes, the small, soft-spoken school-teacher.

Whatever the reason, it brought Wendee to hate Aimes,

and this morning to set out meaning to humiliate his rival in front of the pupils of the school.

Martin Aimes stood before the main doors of the little white-painted school house, which was the pride and joy of the county. In his hand he held a bell and swung it to attract the attention and hurry the lagging feet of the pupils who were now streaming towards him. He breathed deeply and looked around; this was a good place for a man to live. The town was not a rowdy cattle metropolis and was getting more and more like an Eastern county seat all the time. He was a small man, good looking in a quiet way, dressed in a neat store suit and bare-headed. The boys here liked, respected and listened to what he taught them.

Connie Hendricks stood just behind Aimes, her eyes on him. Neither of them paid any attention to anything other than the children who were going into the classrooms beyond them. Only the older boys were left to come in now, and the swinging bell ceased its clatter as they trooped towards the school. For a time Wendee stood watching the young teacher, then drew his right-hand Colt. Here was his chance to make a grandstand play for these boys.

The crash of the shot rang loud and the bell was torn from Aimes's hand, hitting the ground. Wendee ambled forward, the gun still smoking in his hand, a wolfish leer on his face.

"How was that for shooting?" he asked the boys, then before they could answer him, turned to Aimes. "Instead of telling them such foolishness as you do, why don't you teach them something useful, like how to shoot?" He whirled the Colt on his finger, pin-wheeling it before the admiring looks of the boys. "They don't need to know fool stuff like reading and writing, schoolmarm, just how to use a gun. Watch this, boys!"

The gun settled in Wendee's palm and crashed again. Dirt erupted between Aimes's feet, but he did not move. Wendee, hoping to make the teacher leap in fright, lined and fired again, sending another bullet even nearer.

Two riders were coming slowly towards the party outside the school, but none noticed them, all eyes were on Aimes and Wendee. The taller of the pair reached down, unstrapping the rope from his saddlehorn, then sent his huge paint stallion forward fast. With a quick swing and whirl that built up a loop, he sent it up to the right, overhead and shooting out in a perfectly done hooleyhann throw, dropping neatly over Wendee's shoulders and down. When the noose was level with the terror's elbows, the paint stopped and wrenched it tight. Wendee gave a startled yell as the rope came tight, pinning his arms, slamming them to his sides. He almost lost his grip of the gun and was only just in time to prevent dropping the hammer and having the heavy bullet down his leg. He lost his balance and was smashed down on to his back, with his legs waving feebly in the air. Snarling with rage he worked the rope loose and tried to get his left-hand gun out, for the right lay where it fell, some distance from him. The colt was just out when the big horse lunged back again, dragging Wendee backwards and causing him to lose the second gun.

The rope loosened and Wendee worked his arms free, whirling as soon as he was loose and reaching for his bowie knife.

The rider of the paint, a tall, wide-shouldered, handsome blond Texan boy, threw a long leg over the saddlehorn and dropped lightly to the ground, the big horse never making a move to leave him.

"Don't try it, *hombre*," his soft drawling voice giving a flat warning. "Ain't but the Ysabel Kid can lick a good gun with a knife. And Mister, you aren't the Ysabel Kid at all."

Wendee studied the young man, not noticing the second rider who sat back in his saddle watching everything with sardonic eyes. The young Texan wore range clothes and that buscadero gunbelt had been made by a master at his trade, while the matched, staghorn-handled Colt Artillery Peacemaker hung just right for a very fast withdrawal. Wendee noticed the relaxed-looking pose, the stance of a really fast man, the air of a master of the noble art of triggernometry.

Coming up erect, his face red with humiliation, hearing the giggles of the very boys he'd hoped to impress, Wendee clenched his fists and snarled, "All right, come on, cownurse."

"Ranger, not cownurse, friend." The Texan's voice was mocking. "The name's Waco. You're dressed like a man, pick them up and use them like one."

Wendee started to bend over for the guns. Then the name hit him like a club and brought to an end any ideas he might have had of shooting it out. Since the Ranger organization was brought into being, that name, Waco, was known throughout the territory as an exponent of the noble art of fast gunplay. It was a name to speak of in the same breath as other Texan masters of the quick-trigger art. A name which ranked alongside Dusty Fog, Mark Counter, Wes Hardin, or any of the other top Texas boys whose names stood for fast work with a gun.

In other words, it was a name which spelled fight, and in any fight Bill Wendee liked to have a considerable edge over his opponent. In any kind of gunplay with a man like Waco there was no edge at all, unless . . .

"Shucks, I was only funning, Ranger. I don't want no trouble at all."

The Ranger gave his full attention to coiling the long rope, ignoring Wendee. The latter bent over and picked up one of his fallen guns, easing the hammer back under his thumb, carefully to try and avoid the warning click as the weapon came to full cock. Yet, for all his caution, there was a click. It came from a direction Wendee wasn't looking. He looked up and met the cold mocking eyes of a pallid, studious-looking young man afork a big black horse. Another Texan by his dress, although he wore a coat, the right side of which was stitched back to leave clear access to his holster.

Wendee held down a curse as he realized this would be Waco's partner, Doc Leroy, and mild and studious though he looked, he too was one of the really fast men with a gun.

"What the——?" Wendee began.

"Just saving your life, friend," Doc replied, and nodded to Waco. "Look!"

Wendee looked and paled under his tan, for his move would have been a failure. Waco stood there with his matched guns in his hands, both lined full on the centre of the fancy buckskin shirt. The guns made a whirling turn that made Wendee's pin-wheel look like the bumbling of an amateur, then ended up back in leather again.

A boy laughed aloud and Wendee snarled. "A man don't stand no chance against you Rangers, you allus works in twos."

Waco spoke over his shoulder, his eyes staying on Wendee. "Doc, you just take this ole Dusty hoss of mine along to the Sheriff's office and wait for me there."

"I'll do just that, boy," Doc replied, riding forward and reaching for the paint's reins. He led the horse along the street, coiling Waco's rope as he went and never even looking back.

Waco allowed Doc to get well clear of him before he

spoke. He saw that the small man, the pretty girl and all the boys were watching him.

"All right, billshow hand. I'm alone now and not backed by anyone."

Wendee studied the young Texan for a moment, knowing that all he had to do was drop his hand, grip the butt of his Colt, lift it while his thumb eased back the hammer, line it and fire. That was all. Just make a real fast draw. But he knew that the fastest speed would be of no use, for Waco was far faster.

So with this thought in mind Wendee ignored the implication that he was a fugitive from one of the Wild West shows which were run by men like Buffalo Bill Cody and toured the East.

"No call to get all riled up, Ranger," he said placatingly. "I was only funning with the schoolmarm there."

Waco's hand moved, the twin guns coming out and throwing a shot each. Dust spurts rose between Wendee's feet and he yelled, then leapt into the air. Dropping his guns back into leather, Waco looked the other man over in disgust and snapped out a request for Wendee to depart for other parts.

There was hatred and anger on Wendee's face as he turned and walked away. For one moment he thought of whirling around and settling the matter with roaring guns. Sanity and prudence held his hand, for he knew that if he tried it would die before his turn was made.

Aimes tried to get the attention of the boys and herd them into the school, but for once they were more interested in something other than his style of learning. He could tell from the excited way they were watching the Rangers that there would be trouble in getting them to concentrate on work after this.

"Thank you, Ranger," he said, remembering he owed

this smiling young Texan something. "I er——. I——that is——"

"Right pleased to be of help," Waco said. "Your job and mine gets the same sometimes. You try and put sense into these buttons. I have to do it with older men."

Aimes realized that the boys were listening to every word and knew, instinctively, his prestige had gone up slightly by the famous young Ranger saying their work ran parallel at times. However, he wanted them in the school and working, not standing outside watching a young man whose fame lay mostly in his skill with a gun.

"All right, boys. Inside all of you. Come on, move. We have some work to do before you get a chance to use the catapult."

There was a rush for the door at the words. Waco watched them go and grinned at the teacher. "Real dangerous things, catapults. You'll likely have their mothers round after you, teaching them things like that."

"You'd better come along and protect me, then," Aimes's voice was bitter.

"Listen, Ranger!" Connie stepped forward, her blue eyes flashing anger at the tall young Texan who she thought was belittling Martin Aimes. "Martin isn't afraid of that mouthy no-good. He is L——"

"Ma'am any man who stands still and lets two bullets hit between his feet is all right in my tally book," Waco interrupted, with a grin on his face that made her think he was only as old as the boys just going into class.

Connie appeared mollified by the fact that the Ranger saw more to Martin Aimes than just a small, mild man who allowed a bully to shoot at him. She caught Aimes's eye and he smiled at her, then turned to Waco.

"Thanks again, Ranger. I'd better go and start the class."

Doc was seated at the desk in the sheriff's office when Waco came in. Hendricks, the sheriff, was seated at the other side. He rose with a smile of welcome, a big, powerful-looking man, dressed well and with thinning red hair.

"Wendee cashed in yet?" he asked.

"Nope, he scared me off," Waco replied, looking at the letter which lay in front of Doc. "Tolerable fierce *hombre* he is. Orders, Doc?"

"From Cap'n Bert hisself. That nasty ole Cap'n allows we've took long enough looking for the Apache Kid and for us to head back to Tucson as fast as we can. He says if we haven't found the Kid yet, he'll send out a real good team to try."

"Now that hurts," Waco replied. "If I hadn't drawed on last month's pay and next month's, I'd sure quit."

"Says the Army's real pleased that you got Hernandez and Torredos, and they aren't riled at us for helping ole Curly Bill get away any more."

Hendricks looked the two young men over, liking what he saw. Their reputation was well known to him and he'd left them to handle Wendee instead of going along himself when he saw what the bully was doing. He was pleased he did leave Waco to handle things, for his views on Bill Wendee were not flattering and he was satisfied now that they were correct.

"You pair can stay the night here, anyhow," he said. "The Ladies' Civic Reform Committee have a dance on, and they'd surely have me out of office if they think I let you two slip by without visiting them."

"Waal, Cap'n Bert says for us to get back to Tucson," Waco replied.

"Sure, but he allus tells us to help the local law. This comes under the heading of helping the local law, keeping the sheriff here in office," Doc answered. "We'd be real pleased to stay on here for a spell."

"Just until tomorrow, let the hosses rest up," Waco pointed out.

Hendricks agreed to this and dug out a sheaf of "wanted" posters, asking them if they'd like to check through and see if they could tie Wendee in with one. They accepted and set to work, looking through. Some were out of date, having been most effectively dealt with by the Rangers, and these they put on one side, for the owners were either dead or making hairbridles in jail. The smiling face of Curly Bill Brocious looked up at them and Doc coughed, then covered it quickly, for he still felt rather guilty.

The study of the photographs took them all of an hour, and they were just at the end of the pile when they heard the deep crack of a shotgun from somewhere near at hand. Coming to their feet they looked inquiringly at the sheriff, who smiled.

"No trouble there. You come along with me and I'll show you some sport."

They left the office and went round the back of the town. In the distance they could see a small knot of boys standing round something. Going closer, the thing turned into a kind of tripod with a heavy-weighted bar suspended from it, looking like a counter-weighted pole on a Mexican well. At the side of the tripod, which was mounted on an old buggy bottom, was a cranking handle and a couple of boys were turning it. The unweighted end of the bar was drawn down and a third boy put a round clay ball in a depression at the end of it. He stood back, nodded to another boy who stood holding a shotgun, then pulled a lever. The weighted end of the bar came crashing down and the clay ball sailed up into the air. The boy brought up his shotgun, swinging his body as he lined it, then fired. The ball burst in the air and the other boys cheered. Aimes stepped forward, holding out his hand. Before he passed over the gun, the boy broke it open and removed the empty case.

"Say, what is that thing?" Waco asked.

"A working model of an ancient Roman siege catapult," Doc replied. "They used them before gunpowder was invented. The boys are using it like a clay pigeon trap thrower."

"It's not easy, either," Hendricks put in. "A whole lot of men round town saw Martin do it and thought it was. They learned different."

Aimes greeted the other men with a friendly smile. Here in his element he was transformed and his lack of inches far from apparent. He was obviously very proud of that siege engine and waved a hand to it.

"The boys made it themselves in their vacation time. Handicrafts, mathematics, care in handling firearms and good sport, all in one lesson."

Waco could see several of the boys held shotguns, yet they were not fooling about with the weapons, all keeping them held under the arm, broken open and empty. One of the boys dashed up to Waco and asked eagerly: "How about hitting one of those balls with your Colt, Waco?"

"Not me, boy. I can't shoot that good, I'm not a Dusty Fog. Fact being I don't reckon even ole Dusty could hit more than two out of three of them balls with a handgun.

"How about showing us with a shotgun?" another boy put in. "Mr. Aimes can hit them most every time."

Waco accepted the shotgun from the boy. He'd hunted quail with a shotgun and for sport in Texas, but not for almost a year. The boy loading the catapult pulled his lever and the ball hurled up into the air, flying at a fair speed and with a curious angling movement, almost like the flight of a bird. He brought up the gun, leading what he thought would be the correct distance and swinging with the shot as he fired. He knew as soon as he squeezed off the trigger that he had missed. The ball flew on, to yells of surprise from the boys.

"No more for me," he answered, as they asked him to try again. "I never was much use with a shotgun. I'll have to get Mr. Aimes here to teach me how."

The boys all stared with renewed admiration at this admission from a man like Waco of the Rangers. He could not use a shotgun as well as their teacher and wanted Mr. Aimes to teach him a lesson or two.

Another man came up. The sheriff turned and growled.

"What do you want here, Wendee?"

"Just come up to see what all the shooting was about," the man answered, with a wary eye on Waco. Then he saw Aimes, in answer to the requests of his pupils, take up a shotgun. Wendee saw his chance to make his rival look a fool, and sneered, "Do you reckon that's hard? There ain't a thing to doing it."

Waco took a couple of shells from the box a youngster held, broke open the shotgun and slipped them into the breech, then handed the weapon to Wendee. "Here, let us see how you do it, if it's so easy."

With a sneer on his face, Wendee stood next to Aimes. The sneer died as the ball hurled into the air and he tried to get a line on it. Both barrels roared out fast, missing completely. Then with a smooth turn of his body, Aimes brought up his own gun and squeezed off the shot. The ball burst in the air and the dust floated down.

Wendee scowled and turned towards the other men. "I wasn't set," he growled.

"You keep that gun pointed out there away from folks,"

a boy yelled. "Only a fool points a gun towards anybody."

Waco laughed and slapped Aimes on the shoulder. "You've got them trained the right way, boy. Give it another try. I'd surely like to see the billshow hand here hit one."

Three more times Wendee tried and failed to connect lead with one of those fast-flying balls. Each time after the ball went on untouched Aimes would turn with that same fluid move and fire. Each time Wendee's mortification increased as the ball shattered and dust drifted off in the wind. He finally turned, handed the shotgun to one of the boys and stamped away, his face red as he heard the laughter of the youngsters he hoped to impress.

"That's a real angry man there," Hendricks remarked. "He'll bear watching. What do you think, Waco?"

"He's all paw and beller," Waco replied. "Reminds me a whole lot of Wyatt Earp. Likes to be the centre of attraction, but no good unless he's got all the edges and the other side isn't too tough."

"Was I you, I'd surely tell him his cinch was frayed around town," Doc put in. "He'll make trouble sooner or later if you don't."

The church hall where the dance was to be held was crowded on the night of the dance, the room presenting a gay appearance as the cowhands, not quiet dressers at any time, came to town in their low-neck clothes, ready to spend a night having fun enough to make up for the long hours of work on the range.

Hendricks's deputies disarmed each man at the door, checking his guns in along with his hat. This was a simple precaution, not because they were proddy killers, but because the cowhand was likely to fire off his gun into the air when he got excited, and the church hall was only just re-roofed.

Waco and Doc arrived, dressed in their good clothes, washed and shaved, smelling of bayrum and looking tidied up after a much-needed visit to the town barber. Both wore their guns and no one thought anything of that. They were just as wild and reckless as any of these sons of the saddle, but they had their position in the Arizona Rangers to consider and would never think of discharging their guns just for fun.

All went well for a time, the cowhands coming and going between the dance floor and the saloon, yet none of them getting over-drunk. There were not enough ladies to partner everyone, so several men wore white bandanas tied round one arm to indicate they were "ladies" in any square dance. Sometimes, when the evening wore on, the dancing would get a little wild, and if the gentlemen forgot themselves the "ladies" were well capable of taking care of themselves.

Waco and Doc were moving amongst the crowd, relaxing and taking it easy for the first time since the Rangers started. They were the guests of honour, and several women who at other times would have regarded them with the same tolerance and distrust as the other cowhands, now were polite and friendly.

Around ten o'clock the cowhands were starting to whoop things up, and more staid of the ladies started to leave. The younger women, flushed and happy looking, were staying on. It was then that Waco saw Wendee.

The man had just come in through the door and stood there, rocking slightly in his high heels, looking around him. The deputies were now away from the door and having a bite to eat, and so no one was there to take Wendee's gunbelt from him. He crossed the room, making for where Connie and Aimes sat talking.

"Howdy, schoolmarm," he greeted drunkenly, swaying over them. "Why ain't you with the other ole women. Don't all them rough boys scare you?"

"You're drunk," Aimes replied softly.

"Sure I'm drunk. A man likes to get drunk once in a while, but you wouldn't know about that. You ain't a man, just a snivelling li'l rat who hides behind a two-gun killer with a badge. All you're good for is to teach kids that gunmen are no good."

Aimes's face flushed red and he rose, turning to Connie to apologize. It was a bad mistake, for Wendee smashed both fists down on the back of Aimes's neck, knocking the small man down. With a snarl of triumph, Wendee lunged in, drawing back his foot. Before the kick could be launched, a hand gripped Wendee by the collar and he was hurled backwards, his feet fighting to hold on the waxed floor. He hit the floor hard and looked up at Waco, who stood facing him.

"I ain't stacking against no professional gun," he mumbled.

"Get that gunbelt off and I'll shed mine," Waco replied.

This was a situation which held some appeal to Wendee, for he was as tall almost as the Ranger, and heavier. He also knew something of the art of dirty fighting, and once into the fight he reckoned he would have enough of the edge to let him half kill the Texan.

Slowly he removed his gunbelt and tossed it behind him, but the bowie-knife was still sheathed at his back. He watched the crowd forcing back to make a circle around the dance floor and knew all of them would want to see him beaten. He watched Waco remove the buscadero gunbelt and pass it back to Doc who was looking on with amused tolerance and certainly without any worry over the result.

Sheriff Hendricks was about to intervene, but he knew that it was too late. He hoped the young Ranger knew what he was doing.

Waco did know. From his good friend, Mark Counter, accredited one of the finest fist fighters alive, Waco had received much and valuable instruction in the art of rough-house brawling. It was a talent he rarely exercised, for there was little fist fighting done in the West. A man with a gun strapped to his side was not going to waste time settling an argument with such primitive things as bare hands.

The two men faced each other, Waco moving lightly on the balls of his feet like a stalking cat.

"Knife!" a cowboy yelled.

Wendee lunged in, the saw-edged bowie knife ripping round at Waco's stomach. A woman screamed and Waco jerked back avoiding the slash. Across the floor Hendricks dropped his hand to his gun butt, but Doc Leroy's grip on his sleeve held him. Doc was watching everything with the same air of amused tolerance he'd shown at the start of the fight.

"Know something?" he said to the sheriff. "Ole Wendee shouldn't have done that. Now he's gone and riled that boy."

Backwards across the floor Waco went, balancing well on the slippery surface and avoiding the ripping cuts of the knife with the grace of a ballet dancer. He was driven right back until his supporters started to yell a warning that he was in danger of being driven into the refreshment table.

The table was half-emptied of food, but a full jug of lemonade stood in the centre. It was this Waco caught up, swinging his arm round in a looping throw which sent the liquid flying at Wendee.

The terror yelled as home-made lemonade splashed into his face, blinding him. He staggered back and Waco followed him, a Justin boot lashing up to catch the knife hand. Pain made Wendee release his hold of the blade and it slid across the floor. Turning, wiping the lemonade from his eyes, Wendee hurled after the knife, his hand clawing for the hilt of the weapon. He almost made it. Waco followed him up, lifting one foot high and bringing the rowel of his Kelly spur ripping across the back of Wendee's hand. The terror howled again, forgot his knife and clawed wildly, trying to get hold of Waco's leg. The young Texan bent, caught a double handful of fancy buckskin shirt and hauled Wendee to his feet, then hit him. It was a beautiful blow, thrown with all the weight of his body behind it. Wendee went backwards, hit the wall and stood there, his nose pouring blood. He got his foot up as Waco came after him, and although pain was making his head spin, pushed hard.

Waco went backwards, he lost his foothold and went down, and before he could rise Wendee was hurling at him, leaping into the air, meaning to come down full on him with both feet. Waco rolled aside, the other's boots smashing on to the floor just behind him. Then he twisted and gripped Wendee's ankle with one hand, put the other on his knee and pushed hard. Wendee staggered backwards across the floor, once more fighting to keep his balance. He smashed into the lemonade table and it broke under his weight, depositing him in a heap on the floor.

Coming up, Waco went after Wendee, his face a hard, savage fighting mask now. He dragged the dazed man to his feet, let loose and smashed him full in the stomach with a right, then brought up a left which flung Wendee into the wall.

"Enough!" Wendee croaked.

Unfortunately, just saying "enough" wasn't good enough for Waco. He was, as Doc predicted, riled. So riled that it took three of Hendrick's deputies to pull him from Wendee to prevent murder being done. Even so, he'd altered the shape of Wendee's face more than somewhat before they got him pried off. The three men held Waco, who was breathing hard, his eyes still angry, hating this man who was a bully and a coward and who did not even fight well when the time came to meet a man who was his equal in size and weight.

Wendee got to his feet, his face bloody and bruised where the Texan's hardened fists had smashed home. He spat out a smashed tooth and muttered:

"You tell the schoolmarm I'll be looking for him. He can't hide behind the Ranger all the..."

The three men holding Waco were strong. They'd handled drunken cowhands before with no trouble. He tore free of their hands like they were little, puny restraints of a newborn babe. Wendee saw him coming, but was too dazed and slow to make a move.

Like Mark Counter taught him, Waco shot out his clenched fist, throwing it with every ounce of strength behind it. The crack of it driving into Wendee's jaw sounded like two king-sized billiard balls striking together. Wendee looked as if he was running backwards across the room. The crowd scattered to allow him free passage, and all saw that his nose appeared to be spread over most of his face.

A cowhand walked out of the room after Wendee, watched with admiration the way Wendee went down the two steps and landed flat on his back. Turning, the cowhand returned to the dance floor and grinned, "Simmer down, Ranger," he said. "Ole Wendee's all tuckered out and sleeping."

Waco lowered his hands, relaxing. His breathing was

hard but it slowed and the savage anger left his eyes. The three deputies who were waiting with some trepidation to try and grab him again if it was necessary, looked relieved. They would sooner have tangled with a cornered mountain cat than go against Waco when he was in that sort of mood.

Doc turned his attention to where Aimes was getting to his feet, shaking his head to clear it. Then glancing at Hendricks he remarked:

"I told you he'd gone and riled the boy, pulling a knife in a fair fight." Then to Aimes, "Relax now and set down. Don't you have no more sense than turn your back on a polecat like Wendee?"

"I heard what he just said," Aimes replied angrily. "And I don't want any man to fight my battles."

"Why not?" Waco asked, coming up and shaking his left hand, working the fingers in an effort to get the numbness out of them. "You pay your taxes like a good citizen and out of them taxes I get my pay to handle toughs like Wendee. It's as easy as all get out."

"No it isn't," Aimes replied, his face flushed and angry. "Twice Wendee started to pick on me, and twice you have had to cut in and save me."

"Why sure, so don't you go letting your taxes lapse none. I need the money."

The band started up again and the dance started once more, the guests not intending to spoil their evening because a drunk got something he needed badly. Hendricks came across the room and said, "I've told two of my boys to take Wendee to the hotel. Tomorrow I'm telling him to move on again."

Doc turned to Waco and shook his head sadly. "You've surely got a mean temper when you're riled, boy. Knowing me don't seem to improve you none, either."

"It surely don't," Waco agreed, then looked for Aimes.

"You forget him, Martin. He'll be gone soon."

Aimes did not reply, but turned and walked from the room. Connie followed him out, but before Waco or Doc could decide on any course of action, they were brought into a square dance and were soon having fun, forgetting the whole incident.

"Now that was a fair dance," Doc said cheerfully.

"Sure, near on as good as one of Ole Devil's Christmas Turkey Shoot Balls."

Doc looked at his young friend, knowing how he felt about Dusty Fog and the other members of the floating outfit of Ole Devil Hardin's great OD Connected spread in the Rio Hondo.

"When are you going back to them?" he asked.

"Not until Cap'n Bert resigns from the Rangers," Waco replied. "I don't cotton to this law wrangling, but I'll stay on as long as Cap'n Bert's the boss."

They were seated on the bunks of a cell in the Bellrope jail. In the next cell a couple of drunken cowhands were sleeping noisily. The doors of both cells were open for Waco and Doc were not prisoners, and the two cowhands free to go when they awoke.

The only reason Waco and Doc spent the night in a cell was that Hendricks found his home filled to capacity with visiting ranch women. There was no bed to spare for his guests, and they suggested a night in the cells would be preferable to going round disturbing people trying to find them some place to sleep.

"Tell you, Doc," Waco began.

Whatever he was going to tell Doc never got told. The door of the office was thrown open and Connie Hendricks came in. Her face was pale and she looked as if she was just about ready to burst into tears.

"Waco, Doc. It's Martin. He's getting his gun out and going to look for Bill Wendee. You've got to stop him."

"You mean he's going to take a gun and go again that longhair?" Doc asked.

"He is and he can," the girl answered, her face flushing angrily. "Just because he teaches school doesn't mean he can't handle a gun. He's Lance Aimes's son and just as good as his father."

"Lance Aimes," Waco nodded. "I knew Martin'd handled a gun. Look at his hands sometimes, Doc, then look at your own."

"Aimes was a good lawman and fast all right," Doc answered, glancing at the callouses on his trigger finger and thumb, caused by much use of a gun. He had not noticed Aimes bore the same marks, but Waco had. "Then young Martin'll be able to handle the billshow hand."

"That's not the point," Connie put in, near to tears. "If he stacks against Wendee, all he's done to the boys of this town will be ruined. Don't you see that?"

"I can see it all right." Waco's tones were deadly serious, more serious than Doc could ever remember hearing them. "We'd best talk some sense into him."

Doc remembered that he'd heard about the things Martin Aimes taught the boys in the school. Then he saw what this action of the small teacher would mean. He saw it clearly, but to Waco it was even more clear than that.

The streets were silent and almost deserted at this hour, for folks were still either in bed or just breakfasting after recovering from the dance. No one paid any attention to the two Rangers as they walked towards the school. Doc watched his young partner's face. It was deadly serious and looked older now.

Martin Aimes lived in a small room at the rear of the school building, taking his meals with the Hendricks family. The young teacher was seated at his small table, a well-cared-for gunbelt lying in front of him and a Colt Civilian model Peacemaker in his hands. He opened the loading gate, set the gun at half cock to allow him to turn the cylinder, then inserted the bullets, one after the other.

He heard the knock at the door and called for whoever it was to come in. The two Rangers entered, closing the door behind them.

"Just what the hell are you thinking of doing?" Waco asked.

"That thing won't get you anywhere, Martin," Doc went on, looking at the Colt and knowing it was worked on to give that extra speed so vitally necessary. "We know who you are, but that won't settle anything."

"I know what I'm doing." Aimes's tones were brittle and hard. "The boys and everyone in town thinks I'm a coward who needs someone to fight his battles for him."

"Wash hawg," Waco snapped. "Ain't nobody thinks that at all."

"First Wendee fired at me in the street, then he knocked me down at the dance, and I never did a thing to defend myself either time."

"What should you do?" Waco asked. "All the time you've been teaching those buttons to respect the law and that a gun doesn't buy a man anything but trouble. You've taught them that every two-bit gunslick with a fast trigger isn't somebody to look up to as a hero. You taught them that a shooting scrape is stupid and nothing to be proud of. Then because some loud-mouthed, no-good drunk slaps you at a dance, you aim to make all you've taught them look like a lie."

"I've got my pride."

"Pride?" The word came out bitter as gall from Waco's mouth. "Mister, I had my pride, too. I was proud, real

proud. So I killed a man when I was just thirteen. I was proud of that: it made me like Bad Bill Longley and Wes Hardin. I thought a man with a fast gun was a gawd. Then I met the one man who was better than the best with a gun. He taught me a gun was nothing to be proud of; it was the man who carried it that counted. I was seventeen when I learned that, but I'd killed four more men by that time, two of them for no good reason at all. Mister, those kids in your school are learning what it took me four years and five killings to learn. You taught them that lesson, made them believe it was true, and now you're going out there and make a liar of your teaching."

Doc looked at his partner, never having heard him talk like this before or show so much feeling at any time. He could only partly guess, well as he knew Waco, how the other young man felt.

"Either way you lose out, Martin," Doc went on gently. "We know you're Lance Aimes's boy and that you can handle a gun. We know that you could lick that mouthy longhair with no trouble at all. He wouldn't have dast call you out if he'd known you were anywheres near good with a gun. But after Wendee the word'll get out. Lance Aimes's boy had strapped on a gun. Every trigger-wild rep hunter will be looking for you to find out if you're as good as your father. Your reputation would follow you wherever you went.

"That doesn't worry me so much as how it affects those buttons who come to this school here," Waco snapped. "Sure, you could get out here into the street and down Wendee in a straight draw and shoot. Then all you'd have to do was wait for the next one, and the one after that. You're going to have to kill time and again until one of them beats you. After a couple of killings you'll get a big name and those kids who respect you are going to want to follow the way you lead. Mister, I know what it is. I've been through it. One time I tried to get on a trail-drive headed for Abilene just to make Hickok back down like Wes Hardin done it. It wasn't until Dusty Fog showed me there was more to respect than toting a fast gun that I learned my lesson. I don't want to see those kids going the way I was headed; they wouldn't have any chance of getting back again."

The three men were silent again, looking at each other. Aimes realized that Waco had said more than ever before in his life and spoken from his heart. In his mind's eye the teacher could see Waco as he once was, a sullen, hard-eyed youngster with a log-sized chip on his shoulder and the desire to be known as the fastest gun alive. The change now was something to give pause to a man, to make him think twice before doing something his every instinct told him would be ruinous and stupid.

"Can you handle a shotgun?"

"Shot quail on the wing more than once, back in Texas," Doc answered for his friend. "He's just out of practice, but give him a few more shots and he'd have started hitting the balls for you."

"And yet he let the boys think I was better than him with a shotgun."

"You likely are," Waco answered. "I never yet saw a man who could handle a scatter as well as you do."

Aimes looked at the young face, seeing it relax again, and then he lifted the Colt from the table. Hefting it in his hand, he smiled at the two Rangers.

"I used to practice for three hours every day with this gun, learning how to use it. Then when father went under fighting a bunch of outlaws, mother made me give my word I'd never use it again. I nearly broke my word. Thanks for talking sense into me. I always knew Wendee for what he was, and I don't think he would face any man who he knew was either equal or better than himself."

"Not him," Doc agreed. "He wants an edge in any fight."

"That's what I thought." Aimes looked across the room to a rack in the corner where the dull blued barrels of several shotguns showed. "I want you to do something for me."

The two Texans listened to Aimes, and when the teacher finished speaking Doc Leroy rose, held out his hand and said, "Shake. I always thought the boy here was loco, but you're worse than him."

Waco's admiration was plain in his eyes when he saw Aimes was determined to go through with his plan. The deadly risk involved was not taken rashly by a man who was seething with anger. It was made coolly and calculatingly, shrewd and showing not only real courage, but a keen insight into the working of an enemy's mind."

"All right, we'll do it," he said, but he decided that there would be stops he wanted to make before carrying out Aimes's instructions. At the door he halted and looked back. "I'd have put a bullet through your gun arm rather than let you face him like you wanted."

Wendee felt a distinct coolness towards himself as he came downstairs. His face was marked by the fight and his broken nose was giving him trouble, although the town doctor had done what he could for it. He was passing the desk when the clerk informed him that his room was booked for the following day and that he could be ready to pull out as soon as convenient, whether it was convenient or not. Wendee bit down a snarl of anger, for on the top of the desk was a Colt Storekeeper and the clerk's hand was near it, while his face showed grim determination.

"Why, you——," he began.

"Anyways, don't see that you'll be needing the room after this morning," the clerk remarked. "Soon's I heard, I knew I could book it for tomorrow."

"Heard what?" Wendee snarled.

"Martin Aimes is going to come looking for you soon."

Wendee could hardly believe his ears. The school-teacher was actually going to give him the chance he wanted? If Aimes was passing that word around, the Rangers would not be able to interfere. Turning with a curse he stamped out of the door and along the street. At the Black Cat Cafe he stopped, staring at the owner of the livery barn and the horse the oldster was fastening to the hitching-rail.

"What you doing with my hoss?" he asked.

"Thought you'd want it to get out of town on," the old-ster replied.

"I'm not leaving town," Wendee answered grimly.

"I would be, if Martin Aimes was looking for me thata-ways," the oldster remarked. "I'm sure glad you paid up until the end of the week."

"What ways?" Wendee asked. But the oldster was walk-ing away.

Wondering what was happening, Wendee entered the cafe. He saw men looking at him, and the owner came over.

"Anything special I can get for you, Wendee?" he asked.

"What you mean?" Wendee was under no delusions about how popular he was.

"Allus heard a condemned man could eat what he liked just afore——" the owner of the cafe began, then stopped. "Sorry, shouldn't have said that. You might not be meaning to stop and fight when you know."

"Know what?" Wendee's voice rose to a half scream. "What's going on round here?"

"Morning, Wendee."

Waco and Doc stood at the door of the cafe, the latter with a ten-gauge shotgun under his arm. They crossed the room and looked Wendee over, then Waco requested the man to remove his belt.

"What for?"

"I don't trust you to play fair," Waco replied. "Come on, take it off. Martin Aimes is waiting for you in the street and he wants to get the school started on time."

"Without my guns?" Wendee snarled.

"Why sure," Doc replied. "See, he's the challenged party and that gives him the choice of weapon under the code duello. He's picked shotguns."

Wendee looked at the ten-gauge shotgun Doc held, then up at the expressionless face of the Texan. Doc broke the shotgun and Waco produced a brand new, unopened box of shells. "Take your pick of them," he told Wendee. "We don't want you thinking you haven't a chance, even if you haven't."

Wendee held down his snarl of refusal. He opened the box and took out two of the shells, noting they were un-tampered with and each loaded with nine buckshot, a mur-derous charge. He shoved the shells into the breech and snapped it closed. Then laying the shotgun on the bar, he removed his belt and bowie-knife, laying them on one side.

"Your rifle's in the saddleboot, but not loaded," Waco remarked. "Not that you'll be needing it."

Wendee did not catch the import of the words at first. He knew his time in Bellrope was almost up. His money would soon be gone and he would head east to make some more before finding another small and peaceful town to lay up in. All he needed to do now was walk out there, drop the milkcow school-teacher, and light out of town fast. He would have liked to drop the young Ranger as well, but that would be far too risky an undertaking for him.

"You're going to see a dead schoolmarm," he sneered.

"Don't know about that," Waco answered. "You didn't stack no higher than one white chip against him the last time."

"Say one thing though," Doc put in. "You aren't as yeller as I made you in the first place. I wouldn't want to face young Martin with a shotgun."

"Never seen a better hand with a scatter than him," Waco agreed cheerfully.

"Can't say I like shotgun shootings though," Doc drawled. "Makes a helluva mess. 'Course there ain't much doctoring to do. With nine buckshot you need a burying every time."

Wendee was walking towards the door when he realized what the words meant. Doc Leroy was late of the famous Wedge trail drive crew, contract drivers who would drive firewood through hell when the devil wanted fuel and bring it out the other side. He was known as brave as any man in that wild and fearless crew, and yet he would not face the school-teacher with a shotgun. Even Waco was confident that Aimes had the edge in this fight, that he was going to let it go ahead without any objection.

The door of the cafe opened and the town undertaker stepped in, pushed back his high black hat and looked Wendee over with a cold, professional eye.

"Need a fair-sized coffin here," he remarked. "Just a plain one. No use putting a lining inside, the mess he'll be in."

Snarling a curse, Wendee pushed past the undertaker and stepped out into he street, looking each way. He saw the small school-teacher step off the porch of the school and start walking along the street towards him, the shotgun held across his body in a casual way.

Curling his thumb around the hammers, Wendee brought the gun to full cock and moved into the middle of the street. He could see people watching him from behind windows or in open doorways. It was then the first of the doubts Waco, with the willing help of the townsmen, planted, started to blossom into full size and shape.

How far would a ten-gauge carry? How much would the shot spread at a given range? Wendee did not know the answer to those problems, but guessed the school-teacher knew them well enough. He was good with a shotgun, even Wendee was giving him that. Very good, or he would never have chosen such a weapon for the fight.

The small man was coming closer, walking along as casually as if he was going into the classroom. Then he halted and stood waiting, that relaxed stance hitting Wendee hard. He could see again the clay balls hurtling into the sky, his own shots missing and the quick way the teacher raised his gun and shattered them after his own miss.

In that moment Wendee knew he was trapped in a way he always wanted the other man. Bill Wendee was in a fight where he did not have the edge.

"All right, hard man," Aimes said softly. "Use it!"

Wendee gulped down something that felt stuck in his throat. The ten-gauge felt heavy in his hands now, he couldn't lift it. Sweat poured down his face and his hands quivered. Then with a scream he threw down the shotgun, turned and staggered to his horse. Tearing loose the reins, he swung into the saddle, clapped home the petmakers and raced out of town.

From every door came cheering men, women and children, swarming forward to surround their teacher.

Wiping sweat from his face, Waco gripped the small

man's hand, reminded of one other small man who had the same kind of courage. He could give Aimes no higher praise than compare the teacher favourably with his idol, the Rio Hondo gun-wizard called Dusty Fog.

"Don't you ever pull a fool game like that again," he said. "I nearly got scared loco when you went in that close. If you'd been wrong and both of you shot, we'd have been burying both of you."

"Only me."

Something in the way Aimes said those two words brought the noise of the crowd to a stop. It also caused Doc to reach out and take the ten-gauge from the teacher's hand. Breaking it, he looked down and swore, then showed it to the crowd. Two black holes looked at the watching, startled and amazed faces. Two holes where the shells of the gun should be.

"Empty, it isn't loaded!" the undertaker gasped.

"That's right. I knew he would never face a man on even terms."

The boys of the town stared with hero worship in their eyes again. Their teacher was a man, and they were proud of him. Men like Waco and Doc Leroy were all right in their way, but they couldn't compare with Martin Aimes for sheer bravery.

"Class starts in one hour," Aimes said, taking back the shotgun. "I don't want any late comers."

The crowd scattered, school children tugging at their mothers to make them hurry home and get the breakfast done. Mr. Aimes did not want any late comers to school, and they meant to see he got what he wanted.

"Reckon they don't think so much of fast guns now, Doc," Waco remarked.

"Reckon not. Nor will Cap'n Bert if we aren't back in Tucson real soon."

So, as the children made their way to school, Waco and his partner, Doc Leroy, rode out of the town of Bellrope, the town which no longer had a tough, long-haired two-gun terror.

Raw, fast-action adventure from one of the world's favorite Western authors
MAX BRAND

0-425-10190-8	DAN BARRY'S DAUGHTER	$2.75
0-425-10346-3	RIDERS OF THE SILENCES	$2.75
0-425-10420-6	DEVIL HORSE	$2.75
0-425-10488-5	LOST WOLF	$2.75
0-425-10557-1	THE STRANGER	$2.75
0-425-10636-5	TENDERFOOT	$2.75
0-425-10761-2	OUTLAW BREED	$2.75
0-425-10869-4	TORTURE TRAIL	$2.75
0-425-10992-5	MIGHTY LOBO	$2.75
0-425-11027-3	THE LONG CHASE	$2.75
0-425-11065-6	WAR PARTY	$2.75

writing as Evan Evans

0-515-08776-9	SMUGGLER'S TRAIL	$2.95
0-515-08759-9	OUTLAW VALLEY	$2.95
0-515-08885-4	THE SONG OF THE WHIP	$2.75

The Biggest, Boldest, Fastest-Selling Titles in Western Adventure!

Nelson Nye

_ 0-515-09140-5 A BULLET FOR BILLY THE KID $2.75
_ 0-515-09139-1 THE TROUBLE AT PENA BLANCA $2.75
_ 0-515-09551-6 THE LOST PADRE $2.75
_ 0-515-09222-3 GRINGO $2.75
_ 0-515-09267-3 TREASURE TRAIL FROM TUCSON $2.75

Frank Roderus

_ 0-515-09389-0 HOME TO TEXAS $2.75
_ 0-515-09719-5 THE KEYSTONE KID $2.75

Wayne C. Lee

_ 0-515-09618-0 LAW OF THE LAWLESS $2.75
_ 0-515-09655-5 THE VIOLENT MAN $2.75

William O. Turner

_ 0-515-09770-5 THE SETTLER $2.75
 (On sale August '88)
_ 0-515-09818-3 SHORTCUT TO DEVIL'S CLAW $2.75
 (On sale September '88)

Please send the titles I've checked above. Mail orders to:

BERKLEY PUBLISHING GROUP
390 Murray Hill Pkwy., Dept. B
East Rutherford, NJ 07073

NAME _____

ADDRESS _____

CITY _____

STATE _____ ZIP _____

Please allow 6 weeks for delivery.
Prices are subject to change without notice.

POSTAGE & HANDLING:
$1.00 for one book, $.25 for each
additional. Do not exceed $3.50.

BOOK TOTAL	$_____
SHIPPING & HANDLING	$_____
APPLICABLE SALES TAX (CA, NJ, NY, PA)	$_____
TOTAL AMOUNT DUE	$_____
PAYABLE IN US FUNDS. (No cash orders accepted.)	